The Lord of
the Dreaming Globe

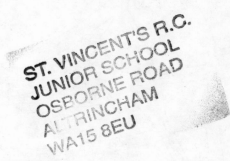

"These exciting stories are a marvellous blend of fact and fiction depicting life between 1483 and 1603."   *School Librarian*

"The writing is full of wit and punch, spice and pathos. The pace is terrific."   *The Scotsman*

"Those of you who read Terry Deary's *Horrible Histories* will be shooting right out to the shops for his new *Tudor Terror* range."   *The Times*

"At this rate, Deary will go down in history himself."
Times Educational Supplement

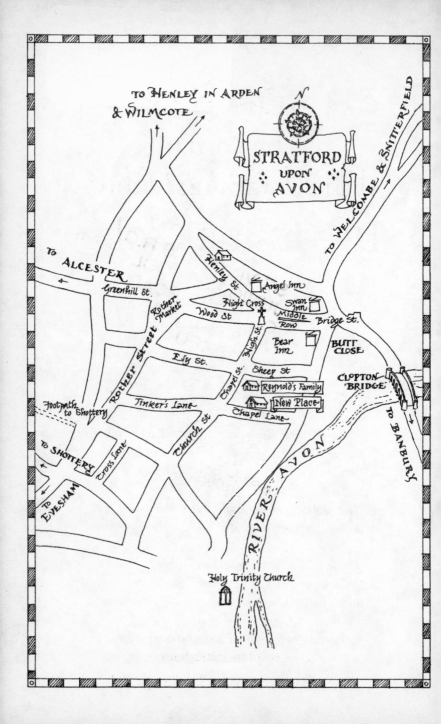

The Lord of the
Dreaming Globe

Terry Deary

Illustrated by Hemesh Alles

Dolphin Paperbacks

For Peter Hudson, with thanks for teaching me all
I know about Shakespeare

First published in Great Britain in 1998
as a Dolphin paperback
by Orion Children's Books
a division of the Orion Publishing Group Ltd
Orion House
5 Upper St Martin's Lane
London WC2H 9EA

A catalogue record for this book is available from the British Library

Typeset at The Spartan Press Ltd
Lymington, Hants
Printed in Great Britain

ISBN 1 85881 523 1 (pb)

Contents

All chapter titles are quotations from *Hamlet*. This play was written by William Shakespeare in 1600, about two years before the events in this story. It is a play about revenge and plots to take a throne.

The Marsden Family

WILLIAM MARSDEN *The narrator*
The youngest member of the family. Training to be a knight like his ancestors, although the great days of knighthood are long gone. His father insists on it and Great-Uncle George hopes for it. But he'd rather be an actor like the travelling players he has seen in the city. He can dream.

Grandmother **LADY ELEANOR MARSDEN**
She was a lady-in-waiting to Queen Anne Boleyn. After seeing the fate of her mistress she came to distrust royalty, but continued to work for them when she was called upon. Behind her sharp tongue there is a sharper brain. She is wiser than she looks.

Grandfather **SIR CLIFFORD MARSDEN** He was a soldier in Henry VIII's army where (Grandmother says) the batterings softened his brain. Sir Clifford is the head of the family although he does not manage the estate these days – he simply looks after the money it makes. He is well known for throwing his gold around like an armless man.

Great-Uncle **SIR GEORGE SULGRAVE**

A knight who lost his lands and now lives with his stepsister, Grandmother Marsden. He lives in the past and enjoys fifty-year-old stories as much as he enjoys fifty-year-old wine. He never lets the truth stand in the way of a good story.

SIR JAMES MARSDEN *William's father*

He runs the Marsden estate and is magistrate for the district. He believes that, without him, the forces of evil would take over the whole of the land. This makes him a harsh and humourless judge. As a result he is as popular as the plague.

LADY MARSDEN *William's mother*

She was a lady-in-waiting to Mary Queen of Scots. Then she married Sir James. No one quite knows why. She is beautiful, intelligent, loving and witty. Quite the opposite of her husband.

MARGARET "MEG" LUMLEY

Not a member of the family, but insists on being included or she will refuse to help with the retelling of the family tales. A poor peasant and serving girl, but bright, fearless and honest (she says). Also beautiful under her weather-stained skin and the most loyal friend any family could wish for (she says).

The Lord of the
Dreaming Globe

CHAPTER ONE

"Thou wilt not murder me?"

WILL MARSDEN'S STORY

In the midnight dark, as the rats shuffled over my bed, the man with one eye came to kill me. I remember every sound, although it happened long ago when I was a boy. It was the year when old Queen Elizabeth was dying and I had left home for the first time.

The latch on the tavern-room door lifted with a slight scratch of wood on wood. A rat squealed a warning and its family scuttered towards the safety of their nest in the walls. There was the soft creak of the door hinge as it swung open and let in the chill draught. It was early autumn, but it was always cold in this damp and rotting building.

The man took a deep breath and I heard the rattle of his lungs. He closed the door behind him so no one would hear if I called out for help. He paused so his eyes could grow used to the dark. He was across the room from me, but even through the sour stink of the old straw bedding I could smell him.

The soft hiss of a steel dagger being drawn from its sheath made me shudder. His leather boots slid over the floor till they came to rest against my mattress, and his joints clicked as he knelt. His hand touched the rough wool blanket and groped upwards till he reached the spot where my heart should be.

There was a rustle of cloth as he raised his dagger arm to strike and the long creaking of his lung as he took a last deep breath to strike with every ounce of his strength. I think I had stopped breathing the moment he opened the door.

I'd arrived at the tavern on the edge of Stratford town around sunset. It had been a three-day ride from London. The horses had been cheap, and the clatter of their bones was louder than the clicking of their hooves on the dry roads.

"If I'd known we were going to ride skeletons, I'd have got cheaper ones in a graveyard," Meg complained.

I suppose I will have to tell you about Meg. My family lived in old Marsden Hall, a great manor house in the county of Durham. Meg was an orphan whom my father had threatened to send to the almshouse, but my mother gave her a job as a servant instead. But servants are supposed to be quiet and obedient. Meg was never that. She could be as fierce as a vixen and as cunning too. Over the two years she had been with us, my mother had tamed her wild chestnut hair, but not her tongue or her spirit.

So, I never dared think of Meg as a "servant" – and I certainly never dared *call* her that. I thought of her as my companion and my friend; she thought of herself as my protector and my guide. She had insisted on coming with me when I set off to work for Master William Shakespeare, the playwright and theatre owner. We had sailed to London on a Marsden family coal ship and had ridden to Stratford from there.

Meg was lively company most of the time but never missed a chance to criticize me.

Now she was complaining about the horses. "I bought old horses because Captain Walsh, on the ship, advised me to," I explained. "He said we'd be attacked by robbers on the road if we looked too wealthy. Good horses would be stolen."

She sniffed. "Good horses would have galloped away from danger. If we are overtaken by that snail one more time I'm going to eat it."

"The snail or the horse?" I asked.

She stuck out her tongue at me.

But for all her sharp words she took good care that the horses were stabled and fed every night before we went to supper ourselves.

It was the slowness of the horses that made us late arriving in Stratford that night and put me in danger from the one-eyed man. As we ambled into a village he was leaning on the tavern doorpost, supping from a tankard of ale. His dark clothes were of fine velvet, but greasy and worn with careless use.

"Good evening," I said to him. "Is it much further to Stratford?"

He lowered his tankard and looked at me. That's when I first saw that he wore a black velvet eye patch over his right eye. The other eye was bright as a blackbird's. "Only five miles. But you won't make it in daylight on those

horses," he said. His voice was soft and he spoke like a Londoner.

I sighed, letting my shoulders droop. "Master Shakespeare was expecting us this evening," I said to Meg.

The one-eyed man gave a start and straightened up. "It's Master Shakespeare you're visiting, is it?"

"Yes. You know him?"

"I've heard of him. Everybody round here's heard of Master Shakespeare."

"But you're not from round here, are you?" Meg asked.

The man gave a smile that was a little crooked. "Master Shakespeare is well known everywhere," he said. I noticed that he had not answered my friend's question. "Stay here the night and I'll set you on your road tomorrow morning."

The tavern was shabby and a sign hung unevenly from a pole. There were no words on it, but the brightly painted picture told travellers the name of the inn. It was the image of a hanged man.

"Here! Let me take you to the stables," the one-eyed man said brightly, stepping out of the shadow of the door-

way. My old horse took a step
backwards, more quickly than he
ever went forwards. I suspected it
might be the man's smell, an odour
as sharp as vinegar. He stroked the
horse's muzzle and held its bridle.

"Is there no other tavern?" I
asked.

"What? In a village this size?" he
laughed. His smile made him look
younger, but I reckoned he was
some thirty-five years old. "The Hanged Man's a cheap
enough place for a poor messenger like you."

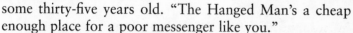

"Messenger?" Meg said quickly.

The man looked at her slyly. "That's right you're carrying a message to Master Shakespeare, aren't you?"

"Yes," Meg said. She didn't want this sinister stranger
knowing our business, so she let him believe that I was a
messenger. The truth is I was going to use my skills to help
with Master Shakespeare's accounts. In return he had
promised to teach me the arts of the theatre and take me
back to act in his Globe Theatre in London.

Meg couldn't know it, but she had said a dangerous
thing when she agreed I was a messenger.

We dismounted and followed the man to the stables at
the back of the inn. They were filthy and the horses were
frightened by something. Meg soothed her horse by mur-
muring in its ear and stroking its neck. It was quivering,
and when she stumbled over an object at the entrance to
the stable, it almost bolted away from her. She clung to
the bridle until the horse had calmed down. She passed
the reins to me and went back to look at what she had
tripped over.

"It's a dog," she said, peering into the gloom.

"Did you hurt it?" I asked.

"I don't think so," she said. "It's been dead for about two hours, I'd guess."

"Ahh!" the one-eyed man cried. "It's Master Ingram Frizer, the landlord, that does that to them."

"Poisons them?" I asked.

"No! He kills them with *kindness*! Most taverners would feed their dogs scraps. Master Frizer has to give them the same food he feeds the guests! He spoils them! It's too rich for a dog, you see? I'll just make sure Master Frizer has a room and a meal ready for you tonight," the man went on, walking towards the back entrance to the tavern.

"Thank you, Master ..."

"Skeres," the man said. "Nicholas Skeres."

"Thank you, Master Skeres. I'm Will Marsden from Durham. And this is Meg Lumley."

Meg carefully dragged the dog to the rubbish heap in the corner of the yard and covered it with straw. The horses were still nervous. "It's the rats," she explained quietly as we unsaddled and fed them.

"It won't be a very pleasant night," I said. "If Master Frizer's food can kill a dog, and the rats are enough to scare a horse, I think I'd rather risk the road at night."

"We could be arrested," Meg said. "There's probably a curfew in Stratford and the watch won't like strangers wandering into town after dark."

"We have passports."

"I'm sure every cutthroat between here and London has a passport," she murmured. She filled a bucket with water from the trough and scooped off some of the scum that floated to the top. "We need to look after one another," she said.

"We always do."

"I mean we have to watch out for each other. But I think you're the one in the most danger."

I nodded. I didn't know what I was supposed to have done, but I felt threatened in this place. Meg went on, "If we stick togther they'll deal with us at a single stroke. We need to keep apart."

"What do you mean?"

"I mean, I'll play the part of your servant. I'll treat you as my master and let people think I dislike you."

"That'll be hard," I grinned.

She spread her hands. "No! I'll just remember what a pompous child you can be at times."

The grin slid from my face. "What?"

"Just like your father! You both think you're better than me because you're Marsdens and because you're men!"

"Meg!" I wailed.

"I might even get to like hating you!" She gave a sudden tight smile and I just didn't know how serious she was. "Now, start treating me badly."

"I'll enjoy that," I hissed and marched towards the tavern door.

There is a tavern in Marsden Village as squalid as the Hanged Man, with villains who hate me because I am the magistrate's son. But the Black Bull in Marsden

Village never scared me half so much as the Hanged Man.

I opened the door on to a room that was thick with smoke from the fire and the dozen tobacco pipes in the mouths of red-eyed men. I felt a dozen pairs of eyes turn towards us as we entered – plus the single bright eye of Nicholas Skeres. "Here's my young friend!" he cried. "Master Marsden! have a drink of ale!"

I turned to Meg and threw my saddlebag at her. "Look after that!" I said.

For half a second there was a spark of anger in her seagreen eyes. They glinted dangerously in the smoky light of the tallow candles. Then she hissed, "Yes ... sir."

Someone chuckled and a man with a blacksmith's apron said, "You know how to keep a servant in her place."

I shrugged and sat at a table. "I beat her every day," I said. "But I think she'd be better being horsewhipped at least three times before dinner."

Some of the men took my lies seriously and began to discuss what they would do if they were me. A man with a face as stiff and pale as pinewood looked at me with life-less round blue eyes. He was the same age as Skeres and I guessed he was the landlord, Master Frizer. "Good evening, sir," he said in a whining voice. "We have pastries made with swan meat for supper."

"They'll be fine," I said.

"It will be sixpence each for a bed and supper," he went on.

I blinked and stiffened. "Oh, I'm not paying for the girl! She usually washes pots, or waits at table, and earns herself a bed for the night – otherwise she sleeps in the stables with the horses. And any kitchen scraps will do to feed her."

"Of course, sir," Frizer said and gave Meg a pile of filthy wooden plates to wash under the pump in the back yard.

The look she gave me as she went out of the door was as poisonous as Frizer's pastry. For a moment I wasn't sure if it was all an act.

Nicholas Skeres sat next to me and made sure that my pot was always full. I could tell that he wanted me drunk, but from time to time I emptied the clouded, bitter ale into the rushes beneath the table.

By the time everyone in the tavern was yawning and making their way home, Skeres was clearly becoming angry because I wasn't giving him all the information he wanted about my message to Master Shakespeare. I stalled every question with, "I'm afraid that is a secret between my master and the playwright."

Finally he rose and stretched. "I have the best room in the tavern," he said. "You can share it with me."

"Thank you," I said.

He showed me the room, watched me put my saddle-bag carefully in the corner, and made an excuse. "Get to sleep," he said in that soft voice. "I have business to discuss with Frizer. I'll try not to wake you when I come to bed."

The rush light showed a bed of rotting boards with a dirty sack of straw for a mattress and a rough blanket for warmth. The dark wooden panels of the walls were patched where rats had eaten their way through. But new holes had appeared and twitching whiskers waited for the light to be blown out.

Meg came to the door as soon as Skeres had left. "He wants your saddlebag," she said.

"It's theft," I said. "He couldn't hope to get away with it."

"He could if he murdered you while you slept," she said.

"That's what I'm afraid of," I told her. "I should get out now."

"Then we'll never find out what he's up to."

"Does it matter?"

"It does if it concerns Master Shakespeare," Meg said.

I sighed. I knew it was the truth. "So, I have to let him take the bag."

"You have to let him," she said.

"And if he decides to murder me first?"

Her face is thin and her mouth is small. At that moment it spread as wide as I'd ever seen it in a broad smile. "And if he decides to murder you? Why, you have to let him!"

CHAPTER TWO

"And dog will have his day"

MEG LUMLEY'S STORY

Will Marsden had a problem. Not the problem of escaping from the Hanged Man with his life. The problem of being a *boy*. A boy is a young *man*, and a man hasn't the sense of a goose. Men think they run this world. That's because we women *let* them think that.

And, before I go on with our story, I have to make sure you know the truth. Will Marsden makes me sound like a she-cat ... no, the word he used was "vixen". In fact I have the patience of a saint, and if I speak sharply to him it's because it's what men understand.

And one last thing: he forgets to mention that, for all my thin face and wild hair, I am an extremely attractive girl. Some might even say beautiful.

So, when we had a little problem with Nicholas Skeres and Ingram Frizer, Will Marsden needed all the help a man *would* need to see a way out of it.

When I said, "If he decides to murder you, you have to let him!" he blinked like an owl.

"Do I?"

I felt some pity when I looked at Will's poor, miserable little face. "You'll have to let him *think* he's killed you. Then he'll stop trying!"

Will's simple face brightened. "That's right!" Then his brow creased. "How will we do that, Meg?"

"You leave a dummy in your bed. He attacks the dummy and steals your saddlebag. While they search your saddlebag for whatever they're looking for, we take the horses and leave."

He brightened. "Brilliant!"

"Simple," I said, shrugging.

"I'll take my spare shirt and doublet and stuff it with straw from the mattress. In the dark he'll see the shape and stab it!"

"Simple," I said. "Your *brain* is quite, quite simple."

"Why?" he cried.

"Have you ever stabbed a sack of straw in sword practice?" I asked.

"Of course. Great-Uncle George has often set up a dummy for me in the stable yard at Marsden Manor."

"And do you think stabbing a straw sack feels the same as stabbing a boy?"

"I . . . I don't know," he admitted.

"It *doesn't*. Skeres will know the difference, especially in the dark when a sense of touch is everything. And when he gets outside into the light he'll see that there's no blood on his knife. Not even a man can be so stupid as to mistake a sack of straw for a body."

He stuck out his bottom lip, and I thought for a moment he was going to cry. "So what do you suggest?" he asked.

"We put a body in the bed."

"Hah!" he sneered. "Where do we find a body? Go out and kill someone?"

"I'll find you a body."

I went across to the window that overlooked the stable yard at the back of the Hanged Man. The window was warped in its frame, but it opened easily enough. I pulled blankets off the two beds, knotted them to make a single rope and lowered them out of the window. "You stay here and sort through your saddlebag," I told Will. "Take out the things that you'll need – your passport, most of your money and a few spare clothes. Put them in *my* saddlebag. Leave enough in yours to keep them busy searching."

He clicked his fingers. "I have some writing materials!"

"You could take them with you," I nodded.

"No! I mean I can write a letter and leave it for them to find! I can write it in a code that'll take them hours to work out."

"You can use the code Mary Queen of Scots used to write to her friends," I suggested. Will's mother, Lady Marsden, had been a lady-in-waiting to the Queen of Scots and had taught us the code.

"They may know Mary's code," he said with a frown.

"Don't be silly. She was executed fifteen years ago. Who on earth would know her code?" I snorted.

All right, so even *I* can be wrong once in a while. But that was before I knew who Frizer and Skeres really were.

The plan to leave a coded letter to delay the men was a good idea – for a boy. There was hope for Will Marsden. Of course I didn't tell him that. "Get on with it and leave the body to me." I wrapped a corner of the blanket around his foot. "When I tug this, pull the body up."

"What body?" he asked nervously.

"The body I'm going to find for you. Then wrap your doublet round it and put it under a blanket."

"How do I get out of the room?" he asked. "Frizer and Skeres are still downstairs!"

"I'll get the horses saddled and ready. You can lower yourself out of the window once the dummy is ready in the bed."

"But ..." he began, thinking of a thousand objections. We didn't have time to discuss what might go wrong. If I had to answer every one of Will's questions, I'd be talking to a boy with a dagger in his heart. Sometimes you have to risk small dangers to escape greater ones.

I slipped out of the door into the dim corridor that had a single tallow candle on the landing. I walked down the stairs and through the taproom where Skeres and the landlord were still talking.

"Not in bed yet?" Skeres asked in his soft voice that made my scalp creep. "You've earned yourself a room. The serving wenches usually sleep in the attic."

"Master Marsden has sent me to check on the horse's foot. He thinks it may have a stone in it and be going lame," I said, as I walked towards the rear door of the tavern.

"He makes you work hard," said Frizer. His eyes were cold.

"I'll find a better life one day and leave him to rot," I said, with as much poison in my tongue as a viper.

"You will always find a job here, girl," Frizer promised. "The customers seemed to like you."

"I'll remember that," I said, and turned to the door.

"Has young Master Marsden been working for Cecil for long?"

"Cecil who?" I asked.

Skeres's one eye twinkled and he recited a verse. *"Little Cecil trips up and down. He rules both court and crown."*

"You mean Queen Elizabeth's Secretary of State?" I asked.

"Queen Elizabeth's 'Pigmy' as she calls him," Frizer replied. "Robert Cecil. He hates that nickname, but the Queen calls him that just to annoy him. And Master Marsden *has* come from Robert Cecil, hasn't he?"

"I don't know," I said. "I was just hired to be a servant to Master Will for a trip to Stratford and back. I look after the horses and make sure he's fed and sheltered every night. I know nothing about his business."

Skeres's eye flickered across to Frizer's wooden face. It was only for an instant, but it warned me of danger. "So you didn't know Master Marsden before you met him in London?"

Then I saw the trap. Will and I spoke with Durham accents. It was clear that we came from the same part of England. If I were caught in a lie, they'd make sure I died too. I had to gamble with a half-truth. "I didn't say I'd come with him from London. I'm a servant on the Marsden estates in Durham," I said. "They treat us like slaves up there. They forced me to come with him ... and they expect me to go back with him. If I could get my passport out of his grasp, I'd be free to go where I wanted."

"Maybe we can help you there," Skeres said.

"How?" I asked, trying to look interested.

"I can help you – if you help us."

"How can I do that?"

"Tell us where the message has come from," said Skeres. "The message to Master Shakespeare."

I sighed and let my shoulders droop in defeat and disappointment. "I've no idea. I'm really sorry. I could try to find out for you, but I don't think he'd tell me. He's a miserable close-mouthed dog, just like his father. Master Marsden wouldn't tell me a thing like that."

It was a good answer, and I hurried through the door before they could catch me with any other questions. The yard was dark, but there was enough light from a quarter moon to find the dung heap and the spot where I'd put the body of the dog. Rats were already sniffing around it, and they scattered as I walked across the slimy cobbles.

I pulled the stiff body from under its covering of rubbish. It was beyond feeling now, poor thing, but it could do one last service to humankind. I dragged it across the yard and fastened the blanket under its body. Then I tugged at the blanket and watched it rise towards the window.

The dog was dragged over the sill, there was a pause and a cry of "Faugh!" as Master Marsden's delicate stomach sensed what he held in the blanket. If he'd cried a little louder, the whole village could have come to his rescue with a nosegay to waft under his sensitive nose.

I called up, "Drop my saddlebag!" A minute later it landed in my arms and I ran across to the stable. It took me just five minutes to throw saddles on the horses, and fasten my saddlebag on securely. It took longer to muffle the hooves with sacking. I was fumbling in the dark most of the time and the horses were frightened. As their feet shifted and stamped, I dodged and tried to avoid being trampled into the filthy straw.

It all took longer than I'd hoped, but I didn't want to lead the horses on to the cobbled yards with the iron hooves ringing on the stones like a church bell. If Skeres or Frizer came out of the back door before we were ready, they would kill us on the spot.

At last I led the horses across the yard. They looked more like skeletons than ever as even the dim moonlight caught the points of their bones. With their almost silent tread, they could have been the phantom mounts of Death himself.

I looked up at the window and waited for Will to drop down. The window was closed. Why had he done that? I couldn't call without waking everyone in the tavern.

I dropped the reins and the horses lowered their heads and stood quietly. I tiptoed to the back door and opened it. There was a short passageway between the back door and the taproom. It was dark in there. I took two silent steps along it and paused at the taproom, which still smelled sharply of smoke. It was silent. I looked into the room. Frizer had his back to me. He was filling a tankard with ale from a jug. And he was alone.

I didn't panic. What use would that be? But a cold hand seemed to clutch my heart and squeeze it tightly. Skeres was gone. He hadn't come out of the back door. It was possible he'd gone out of the front door, but I didn't think so. He must be up there in the bedroom with Will!

If I ran upstairs and into the room now, I might be able to stop him. I took a deep breath ... and stopped. There were footsteps coming down the stairs. Frizer looked up, his hard face almost smiling.

"Is it done?"

Skeres's soft voice said, "As easy as killing a piglet."

From where I stood in the shadows I could see his boots coming down the stairs. I saw his knees, and then I saw what was in his hand. A bloodstained dagger.

"Did you stab him through the eye?" Frizer asked. "Through the eye is best."

"In the eye? How can I find the boy's eye when I only have one myself?"

"I thought you might have felt his face," the taverner said, with a soft sigh.

"He'd have woken up, you fool!" Skeres spat. "No wonder they leave the killing to me!"

In his left hand he held Will's saddlebag. He threw that on to the table beside the taverner. He held the dagger away from his body a little as if it disgusted him. As he stepped into the taproom he collected one of the ale-soaked cloths I'd used to wipe the tables just an hour before. He wiped the blade of his knife carefully, dried it on his hose and slipped it into the sheath on his belt.

Somewhere in the old building a board creaked. Then everything went silent. I wasn't sure that I could get down the passage to the back door without being heard. I had the idea that I might be able to stand on the back of a horse and reach the bedroom window that way.

As soon as the men made a clatter by sitting down at a bench near the table, I used the sound to cover two quick steps towards the door. I still had hopes that the plan had worked. Skeres had said nothing about finding a dog in the room. If he'd really stabbed Will, he would have mentioned the dog's body to Frizer.

There was more noise as one of them dragged the saddlebag over the table and began to unbuckle it. I lifted the latch quickly and started to pull open the door.

"Let's see what Robert Cecil's messenger has for

Master Shakespeare, shall we?" Skeres asked.

"Shouldn't we get rid of the body first?" asked Frizer.

"While the girl's still around?" Skeres laughed quietly. "We have all night to get rid of young Marsden once she's gone to bed."

"Where is she?"

"In the stables."

"She's been gone a long time."

"Probably fallen asleep."

"Hide the saddlebag anyway. We don't want her coming in and seeing it."

"Here's the letter we want," Skeres said, dropping the bag beneath the table. I opened the back door wider and stepped halfway through it. One foot touched the hard cobbles outside.

There was the rustle of paper as Skeres opened the letter.

"No seal," said the taverner.

"You don't expect a spy to seal a letter with the Queen's own seal, do you, Frizer?" the one-eyed man sneered.

Frizer remained silent.

In the quiet of the night I could hear Skeres's rasping breath as he read the letter.

"Well?" Frizer asked. "Is it from Cecil?"

"Oh, it is!" Skeres breathed.

"How do you know?"

"Because it's in code."

"Anyone can write in code," said Frizer.

"But not *this* code!" said Skeres. There was excitement in his voice.

"What code?"

"It's the code Mary Queen of Scots used to write to her rescuers. Mary's traitors knew that code, of course, but they're all dead. The only other people who could write like this are Robert Cecil's spies!"

"So the boy really *was* working for Cecil?"

"He was … and, what's more, I can read this letter in a minute!"

That cold hand on my heart squeezed tighter again and made me gasp. If Will was still alive, our great hope of a long start on Skeres and Frizer was down to a minute.

CHAPTER THREE

"In the dead waste and middle of the night"

WILL MARSDEN'S STORY

When I'd finished making the dummy and dropped Meg's saddlebag down to her, I untied the blankets and remade the beds. Then I sat down to write the coded letter. After it had dried and I'd slipped it into my own saddlebag, I blew out the rush light and waited in the darkness for her to return with the horses.

I thought she must have been gone half an hour when I heard the creak of a stair and knew it was Skeres, come to kill me. I closed the window and shrank back into the darkest corner of the room. There was no time to climb down.

That's when he entered and started stabbing at my lifeless form in the bed. A cruel and cowardly way to kill someone, but Skeres and Frizer were cruel and cowardly men. When he'd finished his bloody task, he left the room and I hurried to the window. The horse stood there patiently, but Meg wasn't with them.

I took the blanket off the second bed. There was no way that I was going to touch the blanket that was wrapped round the blood-soaked form on my own bed. I tied it round the hinge of the window and let it drop down to the courtyard below. It was far too short, of course, but I lowered myself down and clung to the bottom corner. I took a deep breath and braced myself for the drop. There was no need. My fingers slipped at the last minute and I fell. The hard cobbles bruised my feet and I tumbled backwards on to their damp slime. The horses shuffled, but their feet seemed to make very little noise.

I may have been winded, but I sprang to my feet as quickly as I could. "Meg!" I hissed into the moon shadows.

"Hush!" she whispered. She was in the back doorway to the tavern and tiptoed across to me.

Silently, we led the horses out of the yard on to the village road. That's where we mounted them and Meg finally spoke. "We have to hurry. They're reading the letter."

"They can't read the code."

"They *can!*" she hissed, kicking at the horse's bony ribs.

"How?" I asked.

"Because they *knew* it was the Mary Queen of Scots code."

"You said no one would know Mary's code after fifteen years," I reminded her.

"Well, they *do*. What's worse is they think it's proof that you're a spy for Queen Elizabeth's secretary, Cecil! I only hope the message you left puzzles them for half an hour or so."

I said nothing.

"What did you write?" she asked.

"Nonsense."

"Even better," she said, and the pallid moonlight caught her grin. "They'll read it in a minute, but it may be an hour before they give up trying to make sense of it and check the body."

"It won't," I mumbled.

"What?" she asked. Her voice was as hard-edged as my horse's ribcage.

"If they read it, they'll know at once they've been tricked."

"What did you write?"

"I wrote, 'Nicholas Skeres is a one-eyed dog-stabber.'"

She groaned so loudly she'd have wakened the villagers in the cottages we were passing. "They'll have read that by now and they'll be up in the bedroom. When they find you've escaped, they'll be into the stables. You fool! Why did you write that?"

"It was a joke," I said miserably.

"Perhaps you'll stop laughing when they cut your throat," she said savagely.

"Perhaps they won't find us in the dark."

We were on the edge of the village now and the pale ribbon of road unwound in front of us. Muddy puddles glistened in the cartwheel ruts and night animals scuffled through the hedgerows.

"They know we're going to see Master Shakespeare," she reminded me. "You told them that."

"And you told them I was a messenger," I replied.

"Yes, all right. Let's not fall out now. They'll be saddling their horses by now and they'll be better, faster horses than ours. They'll catch us in half a mile."

Somewhere behind us a horse snickered and the ribs of

my own horse trembled under my knees. With Meg's care the horses were healthier than when we'd hired them in London, but she was right. They would never win a race. "So, we hide," I said.

When I was a baby the fields had been a maze of hedges and ditches where an army could have played hide-and-seek. But since then, more and more landowners had had permission to turn the peasants' strips into large fields for sheep and cattle. Now there were smooth sheep pastures an acre or larger in size. Father had begun to do it back at Marsden Manor. "It's the way to make money," he'd said.

"It's the way to make money for the Marsden family," Meg had told me. "The peasants are losing their land, and have to go and work in the mines in Durham, or the shipyards at Wearmouth, or the chemical makers on Tyneside."

"They get paid."

"It's not the same as having your own land," she'd replied shortly. "And they have to live in the smallest, filthiest houses you ever saw. Not that a son of Marsden Manor would bother to look."

Meg was always bitter when it came to arguing about the poor. I'd given up trying to answer her. But here in the Midlands, the enclosing of fields was even more common than in Durham. Sheep grazed or slept in the pale moonlight, but there were few hedges to hide us and no forest in sight where we could hide the horses.

"If we jump off the horses and run into the fields, it will be harder for them to search for us," I said.

Meg reined in her horse. "Is that what you'd do? Run across the fields?"

"Yes. They couldn't follow our tracks in the dark. They wouldn't even know which side of the road we'd gone. They'd have to split up."

Meg gave a smile as thin as the moonlight.

"Wonderful," she said.

She jumped to the ground, unfastened the saddlebag and threw it over her shoulder. I climbed down and stood beside her. "You mean you think it's a good idea?" I asked. Praise from Meg was as likely as a gallop from our old horses.

"I think it's a terrible idea," she said. "It's just the sort of thing a man would think of. That's what they'll *expect* you to do because they are simple-minded men too. If you do what they *expect*, then they'll find you."

"How will they know which way we've gone?" I objected.

"We can't cross the fields without disturbing the sheep. A one-eyed man will hear them bleating and his two-eyed friend will see them scattering."

"Have you a better idea?"

"Of course. I think like a woman."

"I didn't know women could think," I said. "Aristotle, the great Greek thinker, said women *don't* think."

"He wouldn't dare say that to my face," Meg sniffed.

"Aristotle's dead!"

"Serves him right," she said. There was the clatter of hooves on cobbles, carrying across the still evening air. The Hanged Man was half a mile away, but we knew that Skeres and Frizer were saddled and about to follow. Suddenly Meg pulled the dagger from my belt and pricked her horse's flank. It jumped and set off at a fast trot back to the village. My horse sensed it was heading back to the shelter of a stable and trotted after it.

"So now we *have* to hide in the fields!" I groaned.

"No, we don't," said Meg, hitching the saddlebag on to her shoulder and walking briskly away from the village.

I caught her. "So where are we going to hide?" I asked.

"We're not," she said. "They'll think like you – like men. They'll find our horses and start searching the fields.

But we won't be there. We'll be on the road to Stratford. Only a madman – or a sensible woman – would stay on the road and walk the five miles to Stratford. When we get close to the town, we'll shelter and wait for daylight."

"If they catch us on the road we've got no chance!" I told her.

"True. We'll just have to hope I'm right, won't we?" she said with a shrug.

"And if you're wrong?"

"Then I promise that my very last words will be, 'Sorry, Will, I was wrong.'"

"Hah!" I snorted. "It'll be the first time you ever said those words."

"That's because I'm always right," she replied. As usual she had to have the final word.

We walked on in silence for another half mile. We stopped at a crossroads and listened. There was the distant crying of sheep, probably disturbed by our pursuers hunting through the fields. There were hoots of owls and the odd faint scream of some creature in the hedgerow being hunted by something larger and hungrier. It was a night for the hunter and the victim. I knew how the little hedgerow creatures felt.

There was a signpost at the crossroads, pointing ahead to Stratford with the figure 4. "They bury suicides at crossroads," Meg said in a low voice. "They plant a post through their heart so they can't climb from the grave and haunt the living."

"Yes, I've heard that," I said nervously.

"There is only one way to avoid them haunting you," she said. She turned her pale oval face up to the slender moon.

"What's that?" I whispered.

"You must offer to take the saddlebag from some poor, helpless female and carry it for her!"

I snatched it from her shoulder and marched down the road to Stratford. I heard her laughing behind me. "I thought you liked jokes, Will," she said.

"Let me know when you've *made* a joke," I said sourly and carried on towards the town.

There was a faint lightening of the sky two hours later and we could make out the ragged outline of a town to the west. The towers and spires of Stratford were black against the lighter purple and orange of the dawn. There were barns outside the city walls. The first two were guarded by dogs, but the third, packed to the rafters with hay, was open. We climbed to the top of a stack and pulled some of the hay over us. I was asleep far quicker than I'd ever imagined I could be.

I woke feeling thirsty and with an ache behind my eyes. The sun was up and I guessed it must be about eight o'clock. I'd had maybe three hours' sleep.

We climbed down and brushed the straw from our clothes. Carts were already rattling along the road to Stratford and noisy geese were being driven after them. "Skeres and Frizer will be watching the town gate by now," I said.

Meg smiled brightly. "*One* of them will be watching the gate," she said. "The other will be watching William Shakespeare's house."

I admitted that would make sense. "Then how do we get past them?"

"How much money do you have?" she asked suddenly.

"Ten pounds," I said.

"Then we offer someone two shillings for some clothes. We disguise ourselves and walk into town with all the other farmers going to market."

It took us a while to find the right people to approach.

Finally we settled on an old couple who wore hooded cloaks against the chill of the early-autumn morning. They were so pleased to get the two shillings that they offered to sell us the baskets of eggs and chickens they were carrying with them. Meg paid another two shillings for those and the pair turned home like spring lambs in a sunny field.

We pulled the hoods over our heads, bent our backs and hobbled slowly after a boy driving young pigs. He could almost have been our grandson, leading us to market.

We crossed Clopton Bridge and entered the east gate of the town. I squinted out from under the hood. I suppose I expected to see Frizer or Skeres mounted on a horse, guarding the entrance to Stratford. It was a shock to enter the town safely and begin to relax, only to see Skeres sitting outside a tavern, spooning eggs into his mouth. I squeezed Meg's arm. It was all I could do to hobble past him. My feet wanted to run.

When we turned the corner into the market square we were lost from his sight in the colourful crowds. Meg disappeared for a minute and I found her giving eggs to a beggar with sores on his legs that were purple and red and wet.

"What are you doing?" I asked.

"Helping somebody poorer than me," she said. "It's nice when you can do that, isn't it, Will?"

"I ... I suppose so," I said.

"Those fields we passed look so rich, but I've never seen so many poor people in one town," she went on. She gave a chicken to a woman with a baby in her arms and led the way through the crowded market square.

"Where are we going?" I asked as we edged between a stall of leather goods and a baker's shop with a rich scent of new bread. I had walked five miles since eating Frizer's meal at the Hanged Man the previous night, and I was starving.

"We're going to Master Shakespeare's house, of course," Meg said, over her shoulder.

"We don't know where it is."

"I asked that beggar woman on the corner," she said. "Follow me."

I followed.

We found it hard to squeeze past a crush of people who had formed a circle to watch a juggler spinning sharp knives into the air and catching them easily. There was another crowd at a corner where a man played a flute and a ragged bear danced clumsily while children clapped and sang.

We reached Rother Street, which ran south from the

marketplace, and walked down past some new houses that were tall enough to block the morning sun. The further we went from the market the more space the houses seemed to have. We turned east into Tinkers Lane. At last we stood at the end of a road where each house had a walled garden. "That's William Shakespeare's house there," Meg said, nodding towards a long, fine building that was almost as large as my own home, Marsden Hall. "It's called New Place."

She tugged at my sleeve, and led me past the end of the road and into a muddy track that ran along the backs of the houses. It was cool and shaded here. The high garden walls made it gloomy, although the sky was bright above us.

"We'd better go to the back in case Frizer is watching the front," Meg explained.

I followed her and we found a wooden door set in the wall. Meg opened it and stepped through into a warm, sunny garden. The grass was soft and the flowers rich in colour and perfume.

A woman stood on the terrace at the back of the house. She must have been about forty-five years old. Her grey hair was pulled back under a plain cap. Only her eyes moved as they watched us cross the lawn towards her.

"Are you the housekeeper?" I asked.

"I am Mistress Anne Shakespeare," she said stiffly.

"We've come to see Master Shakespeare," I said, a little confused and awkward after making that mistake. "He is expecting us."

"And I am expecting you," she said. Her face was marble cold.

I smiled. "Good. Can we see Master Shakespeare now?"

"Not now," she said in a low voice. "Not ever. Go back across the garden, go out through the gate and close it behind you. And never come back here again. Never, do you understand?"

CHAPTER FOUR

"Let the doors be shut upon him"

MEG LUMLEY'S STORY

William Shakespeare may have been the lord of his Globe Theatre in London. But, here in Stratford, Mistress Shakespeare was the queen and ruler. I liked her as soon as I saw her.

Will blushed as red as the apples in the orchard at New Place. "Master Shakespeare knows me," he said miserably.

"Then you are one of his roguish actors, or a messenger from his other trade. Either way you bring trouble to this house," she said. "Now, you can leave the way you came, or you can stand there while I crack your skull with this broom handle. Which is it to be?"

"We had to spend the night in a barn and we're starved and filthy," I told her. "But we don't mean any harm."

Her hard face softened. "I have nothing against you," she said stiffly. "It's the trouble you bring with you. If you are actors, I'll have a troupe of acrobats and fiddlers and beartrainers and thieves camped in my garden. It happened last year, but it won't happen again. When the Globe in London is closed by the plague, they all seem to float up to Stratford. They drift after

Master Shakespeare like weed trailing behind a swan."

"That must be terrible!" I cried. "You keep the garden so beautifully! And the orchard. I'll bet they steal your apples too."

"They steal anything they can get their hands on," she went on fiercely. "Actors are nothing better than beggars and it's shameful that my husband has to mix with them."

"I know," I agreed. I nodded towards Will. "Young Will Marsden here's the same. He comes from the most respectable home in County Durham – his family own farms and mines and ships. Yet he's seen a group of travelling players and he has to join them. He visited the Globe earlier this year and went on the stage. Now he has the theatre poison in his blood."

"Well said, young Miss ..."

"Meg," I said.

"Meg ... the theatre is a poisonous snake and it bites these men. And while my husband goes off to London to play at his acting, who is left to manage the house and raise the children?"

"You are. Just like all the womenfolk."

"Exactly. If you take my advice you'll have nothing to do with a boy who wants to be an actor."

"His mother entrusted me with the task of looking after him," I said quietly.

Mistress Shakespeare shook her head sadly. "His poor mother needs to be told. She's given you an impossible job there."

"I've found that out," I sighed. "Last night we were nearly murdered. I rescued him from that and now we're stranded in Stratford, starving and two hundred miles from home. We've lost our horses and we're being hunted by two ruthless men."

My story was so heart-rending that I felt the tears fill my own eyes. Mistress Shakespeare leant the broom

against the wall and hurried towards me. She led me to a bench in the shade of a trellis covered in roses. "I was just about to have some breakfast," she said. "Would you like to join me? Maybe we can find a way to help."

"I couldn't," I sniffed. "We never take gifts. I'll never let myself become a beggar, no matter how close I am to starvation."

"Nonsense. You are my *guest*. And you are only here because my wastrel husband invited you. The least I can do is to feed you. Stay there and we'll share some oatcakes with honey from my own hives."

"Thank you, Mistress Shakespeare."

"Call me Anne."

"Thank you, Anne," I said and wiped my eyes on my sleeve.

She went into the house. Will Marsden was looking at me, his mouth open in that foolish way boys have when their brain has stopped working – which is often. Then he raised his hands and clapped three or four times. "Well done. Perhaps you should be on the stage with an act like that."

"Shut up," I said. "You won't be complaining when your mouth's full of my friend's breakfast."

He was about to say something else when the house

New Place

door opened again and Master William Shakespeare himself stepped out. "Will!" he cried. "You made it then?" He strode across to us, slapped an arm around my companion the way men do, and then turned and lifted me to my feet. "And Meg!" He placed a kiss on my cheek. His pointed beard tickled and I tried to look annoyed. "You arrived safely, then."

"Just," I said shortly.

"You had difficulties?" he asked. His high forehead wrinkled in a frown and his large brown eyes looked worried.

"We stopped last night in a village on the Banbury road. At a tavern called the Hanged Man," I explained.

"I know it. I pass it on my journeys to London, but I ride past quickly."

"We said we were coming to see you. For some reason they tried to stop us – kill us and rob us," I went on.

"Taverner Hunt tried to kill you? He cheats his customers with watered ale, but I've never heard that he's a murderer," the playwright said with a shake of his head.

"No, his name wasn't Hunt," I said. "It was Frizer."

"What!" William Shakespeare cried. "Frizer? Are you sure? Ingram Frizer? A man about my own age?"

"Yes. And his one-eyed friend Nicholas Skeres," Will added.

"Skeres and Frizer. At the Hanged Man, you say? They

are closer than I thought. You are certainly lucky to have escaped with your lives. There are a few who haven't been so fortunate."

"They are murderers? Then why haven't they been arrested?" I asked.

"Because they kill in the name of the law. They execute traitors and they have powerful friends who protect them. They will kill me as soon as they have one scrap of evidence against me. I'll be found drowned in the Avon one day, or stabbed in a London alley. They'll say that I was a traitor and it was their duty to execute me. They'll live to kill again. My wife Anne is terrified that they'll come here."

"They *are* here," I said quietly. "Skeres is near the marketplace and we think Frizer may be watching the house."

"I'm surprised Anne let you stay," Master Shakespeare said. "She protects me like a mother wolf when I'm here. And my actor friends protect me when I'm in London."

"She wanted to throw us out," Will said.

"I did," Anne said, as she came out of the house with a plate of oatcakes and a pot of honey on a large serving tray. There was a jug of milk to drink and she began to serve us as we talked.

Her husband turned to her. "Will and Meg came to the Globe earlier this year, and I promised to teach Will the art of the theatre in exchange for some help with my accounts."

"He'd be better learning the art of staying out of trouble and not mixing with vagabond actors," she told him tartly.

He looked around the fine garden. "The theatre has brought us a comfortable life," he said. "Now I've bought the cottage across the lane and the rent will give you all the money you need."

"But it won't make up for the husband I lose every

winter." She turned to me. "Never marry a man of the theatre. Not even a successful one."

"I won't," I grinned.

"I was worried that they might be carrying the message you were expecting," Anne said quietly. "You really should not be putting your life in danger that way, William."

"It's too late," her husband said, and quickly told her of our meeting with Skeres and Frizer. We added the details he hadn't heard and told him how we came to arrive in Stratford that morning.

"Skeres and Frizer were after the message from Robert Cecil," Master Shakespeare said. "You escaped from them, Meg and Will. Let's hope the real messenger is as careful when he arrives. He has a better chance of getting through now, of course."

"Because Frizer and Skeres think *we're* carrying the message?" I asked.

"Yes. And if the messenger is as careful as you, he'll slip past those two as well as you did. I am expecting him some time today."

We ate and drank in silence for a while. Then I asked, "I don't suppose you can tell us what this is all about?"

"If I told you, you would be in danger too," said Master Shakespeare. "I'll tell you when I'm sure it's safe. But I *can* tell you that the messenger is a friend of yours."

The sun was warm in the shelter of the garden, yet I went as cold as if a cloud had passed over it. "Oh, no," I moaned. "Please, Master Shakespeare! Please tell me it isn't an actor called Hugh Richmond."

"It is!" he nodded.

I buried my face in my hands. Anne Shakespeare wrapped an arm around my shoulders. "What do you know about Hugh Richmond that's so terrible? Is he a traitor?"

"No," I said. "Worse. He's a fool!"

Anne shrugged. "All men are fools."

"But Hugh thinks he's the cleverest spy in the service of England. We met him on a mission to Scotland. He passed through Marsden Manor and asked for our help. Will and his grandfather saved Hugh Richmond's silly neck time and again. He is as good at spying as I am at flying!"

Anne groaned. "A foolish man who thinks he's clever. Deadly, quite deadly."

The playwright cleared his throat. "That's a bit unfair. Hugh is loyal and trustworthy. He tries hard."

Anne raised one eyebrow and gave her husband a cold look. "That will look good on his gravestone: 'He tried hard'. I only hope they won't be writing on your gravestone soon."

"Hugh will get through safely, you'll see," Master Shakespeare said, with a weak smile. He didn't sound too sure. "But tell us what happened when he went to Scotland."

Back at Marsden Manor we told stories every evening after supper to pass the hours. I learned a lot from those stories, and now it was my turn. For the next hour I sat on the lawn at New Place and told the story of Hugh Richmond's spy trip into Scotland.

Master Shakespeare had a lot of questions that Will and I tried to answer as best we could. Anne laughed and said, "He'll be stealing your story and turning it into one of his plays some day, you'll see."

"Do you use other people's stories?" I asked.

"Of course!" said Master Shakespeare. "My skill is in turning the stories into poetry. I use stories from history, or from books I read."

Will seemed interested to learn more, but before Master Shakespeare could continue, a servant appeared in the doorway of the house. "Excuse me, mistress," he said to Anne. "There is a visitor."

She rose and looked as cold and serious as when Will and I had arrived. "A messenger from London?"

"Yes, Mistress Shakespeare."

"Then show him into the garden," she ordered.

Master Shakespeare looked thoughtful. "I told you Hugh Richmond would get through. He's a wonderful actor, you know. He probably disguised himself as a beggar, or even as a woman. If Frizer is sitting on our very doorstep, he'll never guess that this is Robert Cecil's messenger!"

"Good morning, everyone!" Hugh Richmond cried, as he walked on to the lawn. He was wearing a velvet doublet of the brightest peacock blue I've ever seen. It was slashed to a pink silk lining. His hose was yellow and his scarlet hat was so tall that it made him a head higher. He'd have stood out in a cloud of butterflies, he was so dazzling.

I suppose many women would call him handsome. His hair was long and fair and his blue eyes wide and bright.

Anne Shakespeare froze with horror at the sight, but Hugh didn't seem to notice her as he kissed me, hugged Will and Master Shakespeare and exclaimed loudly that he had never been so pleased to see anyone in his life. Finally he turned to Anne, swept his hat off and gave a

bow that would have been fit for a queen. He replaced the hat at an angle.

"A fine disguise you have there, Master Richmond," Anne said.

"Disguise? My dear lady, these hats are the height of fashion in London. But the Stratford peasants looked at me as if I had flown down from the moon!"

"I wonder why?" she asked sourly. "Are you aware that there are two men looking for Secretary Cecil's messenger? If you had ridden through the streets with bells on your horse you couldn't have attracted more attention. I don't know why they didn't stop you and steal your message."

"Aha, Mistress Anne, that is where Secretary Cecil's plan is so cunning. The message is in here!" he said tapping his head.

"You are carrying the message in your hat? They are bound to look there!" said Anne.

"Hah!" he laughed. "No! I carry the message in my head!"

"There is a lot of room in there," she muttered to me, and I smothered a laugh.

"It's a dangerous place to leave a message," Master Shakespeare said seriously. "If they find no written message from Cecil, they may torture you to get at the secret."

Hugh placed his legs apart and stuck out his chin in a stage pose. "I would never tell a secret if they put me on the rack and pulled my fingernails out!" Then he relaxed and shrugged. "Anyway, the message doesn't make a lot of sense to me, so it won't make sense to the enemy."

"And what is the message?" Anne asked.

Hugh looked at the playwright. "Can we trust young Meg and Will?"

"You can trust them. I only hope they are never caught by those villains and forced to tell," he replied.

"Then I can tell you. Master Cecil's message is: '*He that plays the King shall be welcome – his majesty shall have tribute of me*.'"

William Shakespeare gave a crooked smile. "My Lord Cecil has a sense of humour. When death is all around us, he has his little joke."

"Sorry!'" Hugh said. "Should I laugh?"

"'He that plays the King shall be welcome – his majesty shall have tribute of me.' Who said that?" Master Shakespeare asked.

Hugh spread his hands wide. "Robert Cecil said it! He said it to me and I remembered it word for word."

"But Robert Cecil wasn't the *first* to say those words. My actors were. I wrote those words in my play *Hamlet*. Now Cecil is quoting them back at me," Master Shakespeare explained.

"But what does it mean?" I asked him.

He turned his large brown eyes on me and said, "It is so dangerous, Meg. So very dangerous. You could die if I told you, and Skeres or Frizer found out."

"I've been in danger before," I said. "So has Will."

Master Shakespeare walked down the garden and plucked a rose off the bush. He pulled it apart as he thought. At last he returned to where we were waiting silently. "England doesn't have a king. It has a queen – Queen Elizabeth, but she is dying. As long as she is alive she will protect the people who served her well. She's like a wall – her rats run out and do their evil, then hide behind her wall again. When she dies, the wall will fall down. The rats will be out in the open, and the cats will get them."

"Skeres and Frizer are rats, aren't they?" I said.

"They are. And the cats are waiting to pounce as soon as the old Queen dies," he said. "They must be afraid."

"And you're a cat?"

"I am. Hugh and I are Cecil's spies. While the Queen's alive, we're in danger. When the Queen dies, Frizer and Skeres are in danger. They have to kill us before she dies."

"How will you escape?" I asked.

"We should be safe in London," he said.

Anne Shakespeare stepped forward angrily. "You'll never get there alive. They'll kill you if you stay in Stratford. They'll kill you if you set off on the road to London."

"Probably," he admitted.

"There's no way out," Will said wretchedly.

Anne Shakespeare was close to tears with talk like that.

"Oh, Will, that's what you said on the road from the Hanged Man. There's no way out if you think like a man," I told him.

There was a spark in Anne's eyes as she turned towards me. "That's right, Meg. Women are much brighter than men. Of course there's a way out."

We stood side by side while Will, Master Shakespeare and Hugh Richmond looked at us worriedly. "Well?" Hugh cried. "Are you going to tell us what it is?"

CHAPTER FIVE

"This play is the image of a murder"

WILL MARSDEN'S STORY

"How will Frizer and Skeres expect my husband to get to London?" Mistress Shakespeare asked.

"By horse. He'll travel the way we came – through Oxford," I guessed.

"So Frizer and Skeres will sit in their tavern and wait for him to pass. When the road is quiet enough they will strike," she said.

"Hugh and I can defend him," I said.

Anne Shakespeare raised one eyebrow. "Hugh Richmond is an actor. He fights with blunted swords and aims to miss with his cuts. Those men fight with sharp swords and aim to kill."

"My Great-Uncle George has been training me for five years or more," I said.

"And how many men have you killed?"

"None," I admitted.

"Exactly. You can fight without killing and kill without fighting," she said. "They aren't the same thing. You may be a fighter, but Skeres and Frizer are killers. If I were them I'd use a crossbow anyway."

Hugh sighed. "So, if we can't fight them, how do we get to London?" he asked.

Anne Shakespeare turned to Meg. "It's obvious, isn't it, Meg?"

"Only to a woman, Anne," she said, as I knew she would.

Master Shakespeare turned his wide brown eyes to the sky and patiently watched the clouds drifting across the face of the sun. He knew there was no point in hurrying them. They would share the secret of their great plan when they were ready. Hugh found it harder to be patient. "Are you going to tell us your plan, then?" he asked eagerly.

Anne and Meg looked smug. "Since you ask, Hugh, we will," Meg said graciously. "If your enemies are waiting for you to go south and east, then you go north and west. You each leave at different times and meet up outside the town on the road north."

"But we won't be safe till we get to London," Hugh frowned. "London's south."

"You turn south later," Anne Shakespeare explained. "Head north to Coventry, then east to Northampton and turn south to Bedford and London. They can't watch every road into the capital."

"It's a good plan," said Hugh.

"It sounds a weary journey," said Master Shakespeare.

"But we could enjoy it!" cried Hugh. "We're in no hurry to get back to London. In fact it would be better if we stayed away till the company returns. Safety in numbers, you know."

"True," Master Shakespeare admitted.

"You have a theatre wagon here, don't you? We could stop somewhere every night and put on a performance! It'll be good training for young Will here and it'll pay our way!"

Master Shakespeare nodded. "I can work on some

ideas for the Queen's new play. She'll want one when she returns to London ... if she lives to see Christmas."

The idea excited me. I'd first seen a play when it was performed by travelling players who'd come to Durham one summer. That gave me an idea. "Why don't we go all the way to Marsden Hall?" I asked. "We'll be safe at my home till it's time to travel south to London, and we can go down to London in one of my father's ships. They won't be watching the port, will they?"

"Would your parents be willing to take these vagabond players?" Anne Shakespeare asked.

"My father doesn't like actors, but he'd welcome a businessman like Master Shakespeare. And Grandfather would be happy to see Hugh again."

She nodded. "Then let's have dinner and plan your escape from Stratford," she said.

The house was cool and dark inside. The panelled walls made it gloomy. My own home had tapestries to stop the draughts, and they brightened the hall. Still, it was a peaceful sort of gloom inside New Place and Master Shakespeare must have had the quiet he needed to write his plays.

He cleared the quills and paper off the table and two servants began to prepare it for dinner. "Won't you tell us the meaning of Hugh's message?" Meg asked, as we sat and were served. The ox-tongue pie with dates, currants and spices was the finest I'd eaten since I left home.

Master Shakespeare stroked his pointed beard and repeated the words: *"'He that plays the King shall be welcome – his majesty shall have tribute of me.'"*

Then he explained. "England has a queen, not a king. So the message isn't about Elizabeth. It's about a man who is already playing the part of a king – that's James VI of Scotland. When Robert Cecil says he 'shall be welcome', it means that James would be Cecil's choice to become king when the Queen dies."

"And 'his majesty shall have tribute of me'?" I asked.

"It means Cecil will *tell* James that we will serve him as well as we've served Elizabeth," the playwright explained. "I'll play my part by writing a play for him when he arrives. Something that will show the English that he is a true and rightful king. We don't want any trouble or rebellion when he arrives in London."

"Not like last year," Anne Shakespeare said sternly.

"The Essex rebellion?" I said. "We heard about that in Marsden, but it didn't seem such a great threat. Essex was executed, but he deserved it."

"I don't care much about the empty head of an earl bouncing across the scaffold," she said. "But I do not enjoy the thought of seeing my husband's handsome head on the end of a pole."

"You were a rebel with Essex?" Meg asked.

"No, no, no!" William Shakespeare said quickly. "I just got into a little trouble."

"A little trouble that could have left you shorter by a head," his wife said sharply.

He sighed and explained. "The Earl of Essex came to me and asked if I would perform one of my plays for a party of his friends. They offered to pay us forty shillings for a single performance, so the sharers of the company agreed. There are eight sharers who own the company and make the decisions – so it wasn't just me."

"Eight heads, but not one ounce of wit between them," his wife put in and Meg grinned.

"We weren't to know about the plot, were we?" Master Shakespeare asked helplessly. He turned to me, "You see, the earl asked us to perform my play *Richard II*. All the plotters were invited to see it, but they asked for it to be performed at the Globe where anyone in London could go and watch it. The trouble is that it's a play about a rebellion. A play where a king is overthrown and murdered. The plotters wanted to stir up the whole capital against the Queen. The play would help them. Of course we didn't know that was their plan, did we?"

Anne Shakespeare snorted. "A play in which a king is dethroned is so dangerous that Elizabeth wouldn't even let it be printed! Yet these eight sharers couldn't see the dangers of performing it. And performing it for a man whom Elizabeth had just released from arrest. An enemy of the state. Can you believe that?"

Meg shook her head sadly. William Shakespeare accepted the comments with a slightly shamed expression. "Essex was betrayed, of course. You know he was beheaded? But our theatre company spent some cold, hard days and nights in Her Majesty's prisons."

"What did you tell them?" I asked.

"The truth! We performed the play because we were paid to – not because we were traitors!"

Anne Shakespeare gave a wicked smile.

"Judas betrayed Jesus for thirty pieces of silver. My husband betrayed his queen for forty. His price is higher because he's a better playwright."

"They set us free because they believed us. The Queen forgave us because we performed for her the evening before Essex was beheaded," said Master Shakespeare.

"Hah!" his wife laughed. "You might not like that hideous old woman, but you have to admire her! She made them perform *Richard II* for her!"

Hugh nodded. "She wanted to watch us and gloat because she was still alive and the plot had failed. Still, I gave a brilliant performance as Richard." He waved his knife, which had a piece of ox-tongue on the end, and recited a few lines. "*If I dare to eat or drink or breathe or live, I dare meet Surrey in a wilderness and spit upon him.*"

"I would be grateful, Master Richmond, if you would save your spitting for Surrey and not spit your food over my table," said Anne Shakespeare.

Hugh grinned, pushed the meat into his mouth and picked his teeth with the point of his knife. "Quite right, madam. Terrible manners. Can you ever forgive me?"

"If the Queen can forgive your performance, then I suppose I can too," she replied.

He bowed his head. "So, how do we get out of Stratford ... alive?" he asked.

Anne Shakespeare stood up and, while the steward cleared the table, she took a book from a shelf over the sideboard. She laid it on the table and opened it. "These are the deeds of this house," she explained, "but there is a map of the town that will help us ... here it is."

I looked at the plan of Stratford and could see the Banbury road that we'd come in on and the marketplace. "There are five roads out of Stratford," Master Shakespeare said. "Two men can't watch five roads. They will certainly watch the Banbury road ... and if Skeres was at the Bear Inn he could watch the Warwick road too."

His wife pointed to the streets. "We are here on Chapel Street. William can bring the wagon into the lane at the side of the house and cross into Tinker's Lane, then turn north to Rother Market. The horse fair starts there tomorrow and it will be crowded. He should be able to get on to the Henley road without too much bother. Meg and Will, you go up the High Street so that the man watching the house has to choose whom he follows. Turn into Wood Street here and carry on to the Alcester road. You, Master Richmond, turn down Church Street and head towards Evesham – and do something about those dreadful clothes!"

"Oh, I say!" he blinked. "My clothes are much admired in London."

"And your corpse can be much admired in the River Avon as it drifts downstream," she said. "Of course they may mistake you for an overlarge kingfisher, but at least they will admire your taste in clothes."

"You think they are a little too bright for this escape?" he asked.

"They are so bright they are damaging my eyes," she said.

He looked disappointed. "Of course, I am an actor. I can play any part – even some dull Stratford sheep-shearer."

"Then go out and walk the streets you'll be walking tomorrow. You should be safe enough in the daylight," Anne Shakespeare suggested. "But take careful notice of anyone following you." She turned to Meg and me. "You two do the same thing. Can you remember the way? Stratford isn't a very large town."

"He has me to guide him," said Meg, and led the way to the door.

We left the house by the front door with Hugh. He turned left while we turned right. Mistress Shakespeare placed a hand on my arm. "I was wrong about two men being able to watch just two roads," she said.

"How can they watch more?" I asked.

"They can hire others to watch for them," she replied. "Did you see many beggars in the marketplace?"

"Yes," I said.

"That's where they do best. They get scraps of food from the stalls, or traders make a good deal and feel generous. We don't see many beggars in Chapel Street. But there's one on the corner of Church Street ... look! He's following Hugh Richmond now!"

A man in a ragged jerkin had risen to his feet and begun ambling after the actor. "Don't look now, but there's another one on the road to the Market Cross," Meg said.

Anne Shakespeare turned slowly and glanced over Meg's shoulder. "Yes, that's Sheep Street. They're mostly cloth workers living there. No one would beg off such poor people. Just walk to the market and back, and see what happens," she suggested.

I felt uneasy about being out in the streets again. I remembered what Mistress Shakespeare had said about crossbow bolts. A beggar wouldn't harm me, but a bolt from a narrow window could kill me and the murderer escape before I had even breathed my last.

Meg sensed my fears. She squeezed my arm. "Don't

worry. They won't be so desperate to kill you now. They'll think you've already delivered your message."

"I hope you're right," I said. My mouth was dry and I felt cold sweat trickling down my spine. We passed the beggar who sat at the corner of the lane, but he didn't stretch out a hand or ask for anything as we passed him. He was a boy no older than me. He carried a crutch, but that may have been to make him look pathetic. It would also make a good, heavy club if he needed to attack someone.

I didn't turn to look, but I heard the rustle of clothes as he rose to follow us. We kept walking up the High Street to the market and pretended to be interested in some buttons at one stall and gloves at another.

We turned into Greenhill Street and saw the Alcester road stretch before us. I wished we could run along it there and then. Stratford was too small and there were too many eyes watching every step we took.

It was all I could do not to run back to New Place, but Meg kept us walking at a slow pace down streets of houses and barns until we returned to Master Shakespeare's home. As we went in the front door we could see the boy with the crutch settle himself on the ground at the corner of Sheep Street again.

"Skeres and Frizer must be paying the beggars well," Mistress Shakespeare said. "They have the wealth of the crown behind them. The Queen's a mean old crow, but she'll spend her money to stay alive."

"There are enough of them to watch the house night and day," I said. "How does this change the escape plan?"

"Not much," Meg said. "I've an idea. If it works, it will make it even easier to get away safely."

"And if it doesn't work?"

"Oh, I wouldn't worry too much about that," she said with a grin. "If it doesn't work, you'll be dead and you'll never have to worry about anything ever again!"

"That's what I thought you'd say," I groaned.

CHAPTER SIX

"An hour of quiet shortly shall we see"

MEG LUMLEY'S STORY

I took the cloak that we'd bought from the farmer's wife that morning and went into the garden of New Place. Anne walked with me down to the orchard at the bottom. I'd remembered most of the map of Stratford, but I checked some of the paths with Anne before I climbed the orchard wall.

If there was an army of Skeres's and Frizer's beggars watching every door, the trick was not to use the doors. "Good luck!" said Anne, as I reached the top of the orchard wall and swung my legs over to the garden next door.

I dropped on to the roof of an outbuilding and then to the ground. Anne had told me the Reynolds family who lived there were friendly enough and would simply take me back to New Place if I explained I was her guest.

But I didn't want to return to New Place just yet. I had a task to do first. Someone was working in one of the sheds at the bottom of the Reynolds's garden. The shed leaned against the high garden wall, the door was open and there was the sound of sawing. I couldn't risk crossing in front of the open door, so I used a barrel to climb on to the roof and cross over the head of the person inside.

The roof had been tiled. There had been a great fire in Stratford just four years previously and a lot of the thatched roofs had been replaced by tiles for safety, Anne had explained. Tiles creaked and rattled under my hands and knees as I tried to creep across. This was the most dangerous time. I was in full view from the back of the house. The windows were dark as hooded eyes and I didn't know who might be looking out. I wanted to race across and drop to the ground on the far side, but the clatter of tiles would have brought out the worker from inside.

I tried to time my steps with the sawing of the wood so that the noise of the saw drowned my rattling over the tiles.

At last I reached the far edge, turned, clutched the edge of the roof and lowered my feet towards the ground. My feet were scrabbling at the wall of the shed, and I was sure someone would come out and catch me like that. If I was lucky I'd get away with a beating. If not, I'd be marched off to the town sergeant and whipped.

I dropped to the ground and dashed through a rose-covered tunnel like the one back in the garden of Marsden Hall, and I reached the wall between the garden and Sheep Street. There were wooden strips nailed to this wall to help a creeping plant wind its way upwards. I clutched at the wood and the plant to haul myself up. There was a cracking and a tearing as I did some damage. "Sorry, Master Reynolds!" I whispered towards the house.

When I reached the top of the wall I was able to look down into Sheep Street. I could see the boy with the crutch still sitting there, but his back was turned to me and he was watching the entrance to New Place. I slid down the rough face of the wall, scraping skin from my knees and hands.

Sheep Street was badly paved. A stream ran down the middle to carry the rubbish to the river that ran along the bottom. The stink of rotting food and the slimy waste around the edge of the stream showed that the people of Sheep Street weren't very particular about keeping their roadway sweet-smelling and clean. When the plague reached Stratford, Sheep Street would be a place to avoid.

I walked past a muckhill that was badly fenced and allowed rubbish to spill into the roadway. Pigs were rooting through the muck to see what tasty morsels they could find. I pulled the hood of my cloak over my head and held it over the lower part of my face to protect me from the swarming blue-black flies.

Workmen were cutting down a tree at the side of the road and as it fell behind me I was shielded from the boy with the crutch. I hurried past the houses with their outbuildings and barns and headed for the river, turning towards Clopton Bridge, where we'd entered the town that morning, and reaching the inn under the sign of the bear.

Skeres had gone, but a little further on sat the woman with her baby, still begging though the market trade for the day was mostly over now. Shops were folding up their shutters and farmers were loading their carts to trundle them back home.

I slipped down beside the woman and lowered my hood. Her eyes flew open wide and she dropped the bundle in her arms.

"The baby!" I cried.

The bundle wriggled and a piglet struggled free and made to run off down the street. The woman caught its curly tail and hauled it back. "I haven't got a baby," she said. "But I earn more if people think I have."

I nodded as she bundled the struggling animal up in rags again. "Do you remember me?" I asked.

"Oh, yes, miss. No one's ever given me a whole chicken before. That'll feed me for a week and the piglet here can have the entrails." Suddenly she remembered something.

"But you're in danger, miss!"

"I know," I said. "That's why I need to talk to you."

"The man with one eye's been asking us to keep an eye on you."

"That'll be because he hasn't got one to spare," I said.

The woman responded with a grin. Under the filth she was young and healthy and her eyes showed that she was intelligent. "He's paying us to take turns and watch Master Shakespeare's house."

"I guessed that," I said. "What do you have to do?"

"We have to watch for four hours at a time – he pays us a penny an hour. If you or the boy or Master Shakespeare – or that one in fancy clothes – goes out, then we have to follow. The next beggar takes our place and we report back."

"Where?"

"At the Bear Tavern," she said. "We get paid our groat when we report."

"When is it your turn to do your watching?" I asked.

"From midnight to daybreak," she said.

"That's good."

She frowned. "But if I see you leaving the town, I'll have to tell him. If I say I saw nothing and he finds you've left, he'll kill me!"

"You're right to fear him," I said. "But what about if you tell him you saw us leave, but make a little mistake?"

A slow smile lightened her face. "Tell him you went in another direction?"

"That's right. As soon as you start watching at midnight, we'll leave. You wait till daybreak and say you've just watched us leave on the Evesham road. Could you do that?"

"Of course!" she said.

I felt I could trust her. She liked me better than she liked Skeres and I'd make sure Master Will paid her. Still, I wanted to be sure. "These men are Spanish spies. They want the Spanish princess to take the throne when Elizabeth dies. You wouldn't want to be ruled by a Catholic princess from Spain, would you?"

The woman spat on the ground. "No! My father fought against the Armada to keep them out!"

"And so did my young master's father," I said. "You'll be fighting for England as bravely as Francis Drake did, if you'll just tell this small lie to Skeres."

"Who?"

"The man with one eye. His name's Skeres. By the way, I'm Meg ... what's your name?"

"Elizabeth, miss, after the Queen, but most people call me Bess."

Will Marsden and Master Shakespeare imagined themselves to be storytellers. But now that I had Bess's ear, I filled it with the most wonderful tale she'd ever heard. Every other word was a lie – if Skeres did ever suspect her, then the story she'd give him would addle his brain. "The truth is, Bess, we're taking the Banbury road to London. When we get there, Master Shakespeare is to perform a play for the Queen herself."

"I know he's her favourite," Bess smiled.

"In the play he will reveal that the greatest traitor in England is a one-eyed man called Skewers – or something very close to Skeres. Queen Elizabeth's agents will do the rest. You see why it's so important that we get to London before Skeres can stop us. If you send him on to the Evesham road, you will have served your queen and your country. Oh, and my master will pay you five shillings too!"

Her mouth fell open and she dropped the pig again. This time she failed to catch it before it ran across to a vegetable stall and started rooting through the bruised apples that had fallen into the gutter. "Five shillings!" she breathed. "That's a year's wages."

"A year's wages for a *woman* servant," I said. "Men servants get much more."

She rose to her feet, stiff from sitting there so long. "You can trust me, Miss Meg."

I wrapped my arms around her and held her for a moment. "I know I can," I said.

I wasn't going to risk climbing through the garden of the Reynolds's house again. I went straight to the front door past the boy on the corner of Sheep Street. I hoped he wouldn't report that he'd missed me going out. If he did, Skeres would pay more people to watch every inch of New Place and my changed escape plan would fail.

I opened the door of New Place and went into the hall. A fire was crackling in the hearth now that the afternoon was giving way to the cool of an autumn evening.

Hugh had returned and Will was working at the table with Master Shakespeare. "Can we leave at midnight?" I asked.

They all looked at one another. "I'd have to inform the sergeant of the watch, otherwise he'd stop us," said Master Shakespeare. "I'll send a servant with a message."

"We'd better start loading the wagon with the food you'll need for the journey," Anne said.

"And the costumes," Hugh said. "Don't forget we're going to perform along the way."

"Master Richmond, you cannot eat costumes. Food comes first."

"But with the costumes we can *earn* the money to *buy* the food," he said.

"If you had to live by your wits, you'd starve," Anne Shakespeare said and hurried off to organize the kitchen servants to pack food.

The four-wheeled wagon was in a barn at the bottom of the orchard. I was pleased to see that Master Shakespeare had a strong horse to pull it. Some acting companies used handcarts, but I didn't want to pull a cart all the way to Marsden Hall. It was over two hundred miles and we wouldn't make much more than twenty miles a day even with the horse.

Will, Hugh and Master Shakespeare were only concerned with their play. They spent the next few hours selecting scripts and costumes and the things they'd use on stage – what they called props – wooden swords and paper crowns, painted gold with glass jewels. They were wandering around in a dream world of kings and heroes and soldiers and villains. They were just boys playing their childhood games. I couldn't believe people would pay money to watch them strut and shout on a stage.

Anne Shakespeare and I were in the real world. The world where you must be fed and sheltered, or die.

We made sure there were blankets for when we had to sleep in the wagon, and food for the horse, and spare straps for the harness and grease for the axles and tools to repair the wagon if a wheel or board split on the rutted roads. We carried a long bow so we could hunt fresh food along the road, and two pistols to defend ourselves against robbers.

I made sure we had a map to guide us and a diary to record the journey. Anne made sure we had a purse of gold that we hid under the driver's seat. Then she gave me some extra clothes that had belonged to her son Hamnet who'd died six years previously. We decided it would be best if I dressed as a boy for this journey. I was not too sure about wearing a dead boy's clothes. "You'll want them to remember him by," I told Anne.

"Sometimes you can remember too long. There comes

a time when you have to let go. I still have Hamnet's twin sister, Judith. She's living with the Arden family at Castle Bromwich, being educated. You take Hamnet's clothes and I'll feel happier knowing you're safer in disguise."

I couldn't argue. My dress was scuffed and torn from the journey through the Reynolds's garden. I took needles and thread to repair it on the journey.

By midnight we were ready to leave. Anne looked at Hugh and Will. "I am trusting you with the safety of my husband and Meg. You are responsible. If anything happens to either of them, I shall be very displeased."

Will's simple face was set in an earnest frown. "I'll take good care," he promised.

Hugh did not quite understand the word "responsible". But he gave his handsome, empty grin, and said, "I shall observe him with all care and love – as the Duke of Clarence said in one of your husband's plays."

"I know that play. And the Duke of Clarence was drowned in a barrel of wine," Anne said sharply.

We stepped out into the chill night. Bess, the beggar, stood on the corner and raised a hand to show that it was safe to leave. I took five of Will's shillings and slipped them into her hand as we passed. Even in the darkness of the Stratford night her eyes seemed to glow with hope. Five shillings would end many of Bess's problems.

Of course, our own problems were just beginning.

CHAPTER SEVEN

"Revenge his foul and most unnatural murder"

WILL MARSDEN'S STORY

Meg must give you the idea that William Shakespeare was a weak man. It just wasn't so! If he let his wife rule the house, it was because he had more important things to worry about.

And Meg admired Mistress Shakespeare for being a strong woman in a world where women were expected to be quiet and obedient, like my mother. Meg wanted to be a Mistress Shakespeare.

Why not? I wanted to be a Master Shakespeare. He and Hugh Richmond showed me a world that I had only dreamed about. And it *was* a world of dreams. When we stepped on to a stage we were kings and clowns, lords and labourers, magicians and madmen. Then we left the stage and the phantoms faded, but the memories remained.

Strangest of all was the way Masters Shakespeare and Richmond treated me as a man. At home I was the youngest in the family and everyone treated me as a boy. Now these men behaved as if I were their friend and equal. I grew up quickly in the two weeks we spent on the road to Marsden.

That first night we slipped through silent Stratford on the wagon. Meg and I had scarcely slept the night before. Hugh said he'd drive the wagon while we rested in the back among the costumes. I was asleep before we had left the town. I awoke to find myself bundled in a heavy velvet cloak. The sun was strong and dazzling, even through the canvas cover. We weren't moving.

The actor and the playwright were asleep beside me, but Meg was awake and busy.

"Where are we?"

"Just outside Warwick. Master Shakespeare put almost ten miles between us and Skeres before he stopped to rest."

We had stopped on some common ground on a hill overlooking Warwick. Its vast castle looked cold and grim in spite of the autumn sun on its battlements. "Will we be performing in Warwick this evening?" I asked.

"No," Meg told me. "It's too close to Stratford. Someone may travel south, and Skeres or Frizer might get to hear of our performance and follow us."

I shivered at the thought of Skeres coming across us as we slept in the wagon or even as we drove along the road. We were too slow to escape him. Secrecy was our only hope.

Meg gave me some bread and cheese for breakfast, and then I harnessed the horse that had been grazing on the common. "His name's Romulus because he has a curved Roman nose," she explained.

Romulus let me place him between the shafts and drive on through Warwick. The gates in the town wall were open and a constable barely glanced at our passports before letting us ride through. By the time Master Shakespeare woke we were passing the magnificent Kenilworth Castle. "One of Queen Elizabeth's favourites," he said.

When Hugh woke, we began planning an evening's performance for Coventry and I learned lines and practised them as we rattled over the rough roads. Hugh explained, "We'll set up in the courtyard of an inn. Place a dozen ale barrels on the ground and put planks over the top to make our stage. We'll parade through the streets in some of the richest costumes to get ourselves an audience. Can you play the drum, Will?"

"I can try," I said.

"I'll play the trumpet," said Hugh.

"What about me?" asked Meg.

"You cry out, 'Come to the Whatnot Inn and see the Lord Chamberlain's players perform extracts from the plays seen at the London Globe!'"

"Yes, but what can I do on stage?" she asked.

"Women aren't allowed on stage, Meg, you know that," he reminded her. "Boys, like Will here, play the parts of women. You'd be fined and locked away if you were reported."

"But on this journey I *am* a boy. So I can be Meg, a girl, pretending to be a boy who's pretending to be a girl!" she offered.

"Can you act?"

"If you can do it, then I can," she said, her sea-green

eyes open wide. "You have to remember, Hugh, I'm a lot cleverer than you."

Master Shakespeare grinned. "That's true. The more actors we have, the more we can do on stage."

So it was settled. Meg would take some of the women's parts in the scenes and I could try my hand at some men's parts. "What do we start with?" I asked.

"The audience will gather in the courtyard. They'll have ale in their tankards and probably mutton pies or nuts in their hands. They will not stand there for an hour and listen patiently. They'll be entertained in one of two ways."

"Comedy or tragedy!" I said brightly, trying to show that I'd studied the art of drama in my Greek lessons.

"Sadly, Will, no. The two ways they'll be entertained will be *with* us or *at* us. If we grab their attention, they'll watch our play with their mouths open and their eyes bulging in their heads. If we fail, then they'll throw the dregs of their ale over our fine costumes, toss their apple cores at our heads and swallow our fine words with their jeers and hisses ... if we are lucky. If we are *un*lucky, they will be in the mood to wreck the stage, tear our costumes from our backs and send us out of the town with their boots at our backsides."

I hadn't been so frightened since I heard Skeres's and Frizer's horses following us from the Hanged Man. "But ... but the constable wouldn't allow them to attack us!" I croaked.

"The constable would be *leading* them. Queen Elizabeth's parliament passed a law in 1572," Hugh said.

"I know," I told him. "One of my father's favourite laws as a magistrate." I could picture him standing with his back to the fire at Marsden Hall: "Common players not belonging to a lord shall be treated as rogues, vagabonds and beggars. When one shall be taken he shall be stripped naked from his middle upwards. He shall be openly whipped until his or her body be bloody and sent straightway to the parish where he was born."

"But we have a licence," Meg reminded him.

"We *have*. We are the Lord Chamberlain's Men and the first thing we'll do when we get to Coventry is visit the magistrate and get his permission to perform."

"He'll protect us," I said hopefully.

"If the mob decide to whip us out of town, he won't try to stop them."

Suddenly I felt helpless. A whipping seemed as sure as sunset. "What can we do?" I asked.

Master Shakespeare threw back his head and laughed. "We make sure we perform so well they shower us with money, not rotten fruit!"

"Can we do that?" I asked.

"Master Marsden!" Hugh cried. "We have the greatest actor in England performing the work of the greatest playwright! Our worst fear is that they will imprison us in the town because they will never want us to leave! We are so much better than the normal clowns and tumblers and killers of calves."

"What's a killer of calves?" Meg asked.

At least I was able to tell her that. "It's a show they sometimes have at fairs. A clown has an argument with a calf that sticks its head through the curtain. Then the clown chops off the calf's head, and it falls on to the stage and splashes the audiences with blood."

"Why?" she asked.

"Lots of people find it funny."

She sniffed. "I hope we're not going to do silly clown tricks like that."

"We're going to do better!" Hugh cried. "We're going to cut off human hands and cut out human tongues!"

Meg glared at him. "I wondered why you were so quick to agree to my getting a part in your show. I'll bet I get my tongue cut out and my hands cut off!"

Hugh clapped his hands. "Exactly, Meg! You can be Lavinia!"

"I'd rather keep my hands, thank you," she replied tartly.

"No! It's all a trick. Look in that box at the back. You'll find two bloody stumps that you fit over your hands and it looks as though Lavinia's hands have been severed. The audience love that bit."

I began to see what Hugh was planning. "So, we do a really bloodthirsty play to start with. We grab the audience's attention. Then we do the clever stuff later."

"Exactly!" Master Shakespeare said. "The first thing a writer learns. Grab the audience's attention. If you don't, they'll never listen."

"So we must be doing your play *Titus Andronicus*," I said. I was pleased that I knew that much.

"That's right. It was one of my first pieces of writing. It's a crude thing, but country audiences love it. We can't do the full play, of course. I'll introduce some of the scenes and explain the parts that we miss out," the playwright said. I started to feel a little more cheerful and believed I might even get back to Marsden without a whipping.

"So, is anyone going to tell *me* the story?" asked Meg.

"Titus Andronicus (played by Hugh here) is a great warlord. After a battle he decides to execute the eldest son of the enemy Queen Tamora – that's you, Will," Master Shakespeare said to me. "Tamora throws herself on to her knees and begs, '*Thrice-noble Titus, spare my first-born son.*' Of course Titus refuses to spare the boy."

"Why would he do that?" Meg asked.

The playwright shrugged. "If he spared Alarbus, that would be an end to the play!"

"A happy end," she muttered.

"People don't want to see a happy end!" he cried. "They want to see death and destruction. They want to have their hearts broken, they want to leave the play with tears running down their cheeks. You have no idea how good it feels to watch someone else suffer!"

"And Tamora is going to suffer the loss of her son?" said Meg.

"She is! Titus's son comes on stage (I'll play that part) and my sword will be dripping with blood. '*Alarbus' limbs are lopped, And entrails feed the sacrificing fire*'."

"Very pleasant. Where are you going to get the blood from? Sacrifice someone in the audience?"

"Pig's blood will do," the playwright smiled. "Remind me to get a bucketful from a local butcher, Hugh."

"We'll be needing at least a bucketful for this play," the actor nodded. "Once Tamora starts to take her revenge on Titus."

"We will. First, Meg, you come in as Titus's daughter, Lavinia. Your tongue has been cut out and your hands lopped off. Just dip those stumps in the bucket of blood before you come on the stage. The audience love that bit."

"But they like the next bit best," Hugh grinned.

"Tamora tells Titus that his sons will be executed if he doesn't agree to have his hand cut off. We'll do that on stage, Will. I'll have a pink glove, stuffed to look like a hand, and a bladder of pig's blood up my sleeve. As you chop through the wrist, make sure you burst the bladder."

"So, now do you have your happy ending?" Meg asked. "Tamora loses her son and Titus loses his hand. They're even now, aren't they?"

"God's teeth, no!" Hugh roared. "You see it was all a trick!"

"I know it was a trick. I didn't expect you really to have your hand cut off."

"No, no, no, Meg! I mean it was all a trick by *Tamora*. She tricked Titus into having his hand cut off to save his sons. But his sons had already been executed! Tamora goes off stage and comes back on with their two heads!"

"Dripping pig's blood, I'm sure," she said with a pained look.

"Naturally! Remember, our audiences happily trot along to public executions and cheer when the rope goes round the victim's neck. But I've seen grown men vomit when Tamora walks on stage with those heads."

"Who can blame them?" Meg sighed.

"And that's where Master Shakespeare's writing is so wonderful! Just when everyone expects Titus to go mad with rage and grief, he simply goes mad! '*I have not another tear to shed*'. And he breaks down into the laughter of a madman."

"You'll be good at that," Meg said.

"I'm marvellous. It really shakes the audience, I can tell you," Hugh said happily.

"I do like a happy ending," Meg said, raising one eyebrow in disgust.

"Oh, but *that's* not the end. There is still the revenge scene."

"But she's had her revenge in revenge for Titus's revenge," Meg objected.

"Ah, but *Titus* has to have *his* revenge on Tamora for *her* revenge on *him* for *his* revenge on *her*, you see?"

"I think so."

"Tamora still has two sons – the ones who gave Titus's sons the chop."

"But Titus doesn't cut off their heads," Meg said cunningly.

"You're right!" Hugh laughed. "How did you know?"

"Because he hasn't got a hand. He'd find it hard to use an axe one-handed."

Hugh frowned. "You have a point there," he agreed. "But he thinks of something much more disgusting."

"What's more disgusting than heads and hands bouncing around the stage dripping pig's blood?" Meg wondered.

"Titus invites Tamora to a feast!"

"That's nice of him."

"And he serves up a big pie." Hugh lowered his voice to a dramatic hiss. "Tamora eats the pie and then Titus tells her the terrible truth!"

"He'd spat in it?" Meg asked. "That's what I'd do."

"Worse, much worse!"

"I give up."

"Titus has cut the throats of Tamora's sons and baked them in the pie she has just eaten!"

"That is quite disgusting! Even the food at Michael's tavern in Marsden isn't that bad," Meg said.

"At that point Titus kills you, Lavinia, to put you out of your misery. *'Die, die Lavinia, and thy shame with thee!'* Then Titus kills Tamora. Finally Master

Shakespeare enters as an ally of Tamora and kills Titus."

Meg blew a long breath out. "There must be bodies all over the stage. It's a pity Master Shakespeare can't kill himself, then the audience will be *really* happy."

"No," Hugh said seriously. "Someone has to stay alive to deliver the final speech. That's Master Shakespeare's job."

Meg sat in silence for a while. "And the audience in Coventry will like all this murder and revenge?" she asked.

"They will *love* it," Hugh assured her. "It'll put them in the mood for a more serious piece later."

"What's the second play?" I asked.

I almost lost my balance and fell off the swaying wagon when he told me. "*Richard II*, of course."

"But ... but that's the play that you were locked up for performing in London!" I groaned. "It's about over-throwing the rightful king!"

Master Shakespeare stroked his beard, pulling it to a point. "Yes, Will, it's dangerous. But someone has to get the message across to the people of England. That's our real job. We aren't just travelling entertainers. We're travelling messengers," he said quietly.

The one-eyed Skeres had already tried to stop that message with his knife. I'd watched him plunge it into the dummy at the Hanged Man time and again.

It was a dangerous message to carry in the days of the dying Queen. I wondered where the next knife would come from.

CHAPTER EIGHT

"These are but wild and whirling words"

MEG LUMLEY'S STORY

When Will Marsden says that Master Shakespeare and Hugh Richmond treated him like a man and an equal, it's not quite true. They treated him like an equal and a *boy* – because they were *all* boys playing at pretend games like children do.

I joined in their games because I would have been bored if I hadn't. But I could see why women were banned from appearing on the stage. The men were afraid that women would force them to see sense. Take Master Shakespeare's *Titus Andronicus*. He might have been able to write exciting plays, but he knew nothing about women. Tamora would never bother with all that hand-chopping, head-chopping revenge. Why, even our own Queen Elizabeth took eighteen years to execute her cousin, Mary Queen of Scots.

No. Women and men are different and Master Shakespeare never got his women characters quite right. But who was I to argue? You notice they gave me a character who had her tongue cut out very early in the play?

All that afternoon as we drove on to Coventry we practised our lines until we were near perfect. The second play, *Richard II*, would have scenes with only Hugh and Master Shakespeare. They knew their lines for that.

We reached Coventry late in the afternoon. A great town behind strong walls. The timber houses were rich and there were enough churches for you to visit a different one every day of the week.

We drove to the town hall with its high towers and its guards in the town's uniform. We were shown into the mayor's room. He was a fat, red-faced man in fur robes and gold chains. "Actors, eh?"

Master Shakespeare bowed low. "Yes, your worship."

"Road tramps and thieving magpies, the lot of you."

"We are birds of brighter feathers than magpies," the playwright said gently. "We *parrot* the words of the famous Master Shakespeare. The Queen herself has called Master Shakespeare the greatest playwright that ever lived."

"The Queen, you say?" the man spluttered.

"We are a small company from the Lord Chamberlain's Men," Hugh said, waving our passports under his nose. "Once London is clear of the plague we shall be performing for Queen Elizabeth herself. And we will tell her all about the welcome we received in her loyal town of Coventry."

"You will?"

"We will. We'll tell her of the fine meal the mayor prepared for us and the way he sent his own guard to help us set up our stage. We'll tell how his worship, the mayor himself, attended the play because he is a man of such good taste and fine breeding," Hugh went on. It was a sickening performance to watch. More sickening than *Titus Andronicus*, believe me.

The fat little mayor seemed to swell up, like a pig's bladder when a boy blows into it to make a football. "I'll even bring my wife and children!" he promised, with a smile.

"And a tavern, your worship? At which tavern should we set up stage?" Master Shakespeare asked.

"At the sign of the Bear and Staff," he said. "My wife's cousin is the taverner. Tell him I sent you."

"The performance will start at six o'clock, your worship," said Hugh with a bow so low that his hair almost swept the floor.

"A fine performance, Hugh," Will grinned as we went back down the stairs to our cart.

"A toad could not have crawled any lower," I agreed.

The next two hours were frantic. Even I was caught up in the excitement and confusion. The taverner at the Bear and Staff was a sullen, dark-eyed man, but when we explained how his sales of wine and ale and food would be huge if we performed there, his eyes showed a spark. A spark that men call greed.

We left instructions for the mayor's sergeant of the guard to build us a platform on the beer barrels, while we stabled Romulus and unpacked the costumes and wigs and props we'd be needing for that evening's performance.

Master Taverner gave us a fine venison pastry to eat

and some sweet pears in a custard sauce. "I won't charge you for that," he said with a twist of his face that was supposed to be a wink. Then we selected some of the brightest costumes on the wagon to dress in and set off through the streets of Coventry with a trumpet and drum to tell the townsfolk about our performance.

"This is the town where the famous Lady Godiva rode naked," Master Shakespeare explained while Hugh blasted the trumpet and Will rattled his drum.

"Why would she do a thing like that?" I asked.

"It was a sort of bet with her husband. The poor people could not afford their taxes. Lady Godiva begged her husband to lower them. He said he'd do it if she rode through the streets of Coventry with no clothes on. He didn't expect her to, of course."

"But she did?"

"She did," Master Shakespeare nodded. "A wonderful story. I only wish I could use it in one of my plays."

"Difficult," I said. "With boys playing the parts of women."

He laughed. "Perhaps one day women may appear on England's stages."

"And perhaps one woman will appear on your stage tonight!" I said angrily.

"Sorry, Meg. I sometimes forget you are a young woman," he said.

If I had had a knife to hand I'd have cut his tongue out and let him play Lavinia. But women aren't vengeful like men. I gave him my sweetest smile. "That's all right, Master Shakespeare, I sometimes forget I'm with three men on our journey."

I would have said more, but I felt a sharp pain in my back and turned to find that three street urchins were throwing stones at us for fun. While Hugh trumpeted and Will drummed and Master Shakespeare called to the crowds to come and see our show, I had a stone fight with the urchins.

But the urchins were nothing to the ugly crowd that gathered in the courtyard of the Bear and Staff that evening. "We have bear-baiting and cock-fights here," the taverner explained. I could see from the hard faces of the unshaven, greasy men that they wanted another bloody spectacle that night. If we didn't entertain them with our plays, they would have their fun another way.

We stood behind a doorway where we'd hung a curtain. This was where we'd make our entrances. We took turns peering out to see the audience crowding into the yard. Most held tankards of ale and many seemed to be on their tenth tankard of the evening. A few better-dressed gentlemen with their ladies took up their positions on the balconies that led out from the upstairs rooms of the tavern. "They'll have a better view and be away from the jostling and the smell of the groundlings," Hugh explained. "Don't forget to carry the collecting cap up there when we've finished."

I looked at the red-eyed, wet-mouthed, sneering faces of the groundlings and wondered if we would be allowed to finish. Will was pale as a swan's feather and I realized he was terrified. I noticed that the curtain that I was holding in my hand was quivering. My own hand was shaking and I hadn't noticed. That's when I knew that I was terrified too.

Hugh's eyes were bright with excitement and even Master Shakespeare was pacing up and down the corridor as we waited to enter.

I gripped the curtain tighter to stop my hand shaking. There was a stir in the audience and the mayor in his robes pushed his way to the front. He climbed the steps up to the stage and made a speech to the mob. They listened for a little while, but when he started to thank the taverner and the pot boys and the cleaners at the Bear and Staff, they became bored. Someone shouted, "Get off the scaffold or we'll hang you!" and the mayor began arguing furiously.

Hugh's jaw was set tight and he murmured, "Yes, get off, you little idiot! Don't stir them up before we've even started!"

The mayor was finally shouted down and he waddled off to take his place in one of the galleries in the centre. Master Shakespeare took a deep breath, said, "Good luck, everyone," and ran out on to the stage in his glittering cloth of gold costume. He introduced the play in a ringing voice that held the crowd like a magician casting a spell. The ugly, red-eyed faces were turned up to him in wonder. The wet mouths forgot to sup at the ale and hung open, showing black, yellow and green teeth. The vicious faces gaped like innocent children at a fireside tale.

I'd seen plays before, but I'd never seen an audience from the stage. The watchers gasped when I was led on, wriststumps dripping blood. I'll swear that there were tears in those hard eyes when Titus killed me and I died in pitiful, tongue-less silence.

After the murder of Tamora (which was cheered wildly by the audience) and the assassination of Titus (met by groans) we rose from the dead and took our bow.

Master Shakespeare quickly changed his costume while Hugh performed a song with his lute. The playwright returned to play King Richard and Hugh threw on a new cloak and doublet to play his enemy, Henry Bolingbroke.

My part was finished. I pulled off the long wig and dress which were both damp with sweat although the sun had fallen below the roof of the tavern and it was a cool-enough evening. Will too had pulled off his wig and sank exhausted on the lid of a costume trunk. "Did I dream that?" he asked.

"No," I said. Now, I have always tried to keep Will Marsden in the real world by being a little harsh with him. But his flushed face was so happy I hadn't the heart to break his fantasy. Instead I simply said, "You were good, Will. You'll make a fine actor."

He looked at me uncertainly. "Do you mean that?"

"Do I lie to you, Will?"

"No, Meg."

"I can see why you want to be an actor, Will."

"It's exciting on that stage, isn't it?"

"Just for an hour or so the audience can forget all their troubles – their struggles to make money, their sickness and their anger and their unhappiness," I said. "It's a powerful thing, this theatre."

There was a roar from the courtyard as Master Shakespeare finally died as Richard. I looked through the curtain. Those cruel, hostile faces were relaxed and happy.

Hugh and the playwright were taking a bow and they were being showered with coins. I snatched a cap and hurried on stage to pick up the money. Then I went into the audience to collect more.

Men and women were talking excitedly about what they'd just seen. When I went into the galleries with the gentlemen and ladies I heard more disturbing talk. I caught the name "Elizabeth" and stepped back into the shadows. "Those actors are playing a dangerous game – showing a play about a king being dethroned," a man in a suit of rich brown velvet was saying.

"Especially at a time like this," his friend, a white-bearded man in black, agreed.

"But it makes you think," the first man said.

"That's what's so dangerous," the other answered.

I stepped forward and asked, "Would you like to give a little money for the actors, sirs?"

They both reached into their purses and took out a handful of coins, then dropped them carelessly into the cap. "There you are, boy," the older one said. "A fine show."

I bowed and backed out of the room, the cap heavy with money, and went back down to the room we'd used as a dressing room. The other three "boys" were laughing and congratulating one another, sharing the moments when things on stage had looked tricky – when Titus had his hand severed and it dropped off a second or two before the blood bag split.

All the fear they'd had before the performance was gone. Everything was right with the world – even the money was more than they had expected.

It was well after dark before we had the costumes packed and stowed safely in the cart, ready for an early start the next day. The miserable landlord managed to find us some rooms in the attic so we wouldn't be sleeping on costumes in the wagon, or with the horse.

I was quite exhausted yet unable to sleep for hours. The night noises faded as the customers went home. Rats rattled and squeaked beneath the floorboards, and pigeons in a nearby loft cooed too loudly. But it wasn't the noise that kept me awake. It was the excitement of knowing we'd be doing it all over again the next day in Leicester. It was the fear of knowing the next audience might not be so kind.

Every day was different – travelling through forests and villages, each with its own story. "Robin Hood lived here," Master Shakespeare told me as we approached Nottingham two days later. Every day we had a new mayor to persuade, a new innkeeper to deal with and a new audience to win over.

And every day was the *same*. The slow build-up of excitement till we were about to go on stage. The terror of those first steps, the excitement of the performance, then the exhaustion at the final bow. On Sundays when we weren't allowed to perform, the days were hollow as a tomb. We rehearsed new scenes and let Romulus rest.

The days passed in a dream. The longer the dream went on, the more the nightmare faded; the nightmare of a one-eyed man and a dagger. The further north we headed, the wilder the countryside became. The parklands and deer forests gave way to scrubland and moors. After we left

Doncaster and its mighty cathedral we travelled an hour without seeing another person on the road.

The weather grew colder as we got further north and further into the autumn. But Will and I were heading home. We went through Richmond because Hugh wanted to see the town where his family came from. It meant a delay in reaching Durham, and Will and I were becoming impatient.

We could have reached Marsden and home two weeks to the day after we set off from Stratford. Instead we stopped at the city of Durham and performed in the market square for one of our largest crowds. They rarely saw proper plays this far north – only small pageants and travelling acrobats or musicians. It was in Durham that the mayor and his council took the performance of *Richard II* most seriously.

The mayor, a man with watery grey eyes and an untidy beard, told Master Shakespeare, "We are afraid of the Queen dying. We know we aren't supposed to discuss it – the Queen would be angry – but we talk about little else."

"You are afraid the Scots might invade?" Hugh asked.

"We are *sure* they will invade," the mayor sighed. "If James VI of Scotland isn't offered the English throne, he'll bring down an army and take it. The people of the north will suffer the most when that happens."

"I know," Hugh Richmond said.

"Your play is a warning," the mayor went on. "A warning of what happens when a monarch is too weak."

"Elizabeth is strong," Master Shakespeare said carefully.

"Then let her name King James VI as the next English king."

The playwright shook his head slowly. "She won't do that. She would be admitting that she is going to die soon."

"But she *is* going to die soon!"

"She refuses to believe it."

The mayor waved his hand in an impatient gesture. "Then maybe you should perform your play for her."

Master Shakespeare managed to smother a smile. "And maybe we would be locked in prison if we did."

"Aye," the mayor of Durham said, letting his shoulders sag. "It's a dangerous thing you're doing."

The nightmare had been forgotten for two weeks. The closer we got to home the closer we came to the memory of the one-eyed killer.

Of course, we knew Skeres and Frizer were two hundred miles away or more, searching for us in the south of England. Of course, we knew that the nearer we got to Marsden Hall the safer we would be.

Of course ... even the best laid plans can go wrong. Even I, Meg Lumley, can be wrong once in a while.

CHAPTER NINE

"How shall this bloody deed be answered?"

WILL MARSDEN'S STORY

I can't blame Meg. I know that she and Mistress Shakespeare had thought of the plan for us to go home to Marsden Manor. But Hugh and Master Shakespeare and I had all agreed it should keep us safe until we could get to London.

We thought we had played our last performance on the road. We were relaxed and travelling slowly along the Newcastle road towards my home. The trees were turning gold, red and flame-orange in the clear light of the morning. Master Shakespeare was asking about my family whom he was about to meet and I was trying to tell him.

"Of course, my grandfather, Sir Clifford Marsden, is the senior member of the family."

"But your grandmother would argue with that!" Meg interrupted.

"My *grandfather*," I repeated firmly, "fought in the wars against the Scots. You like collecting stories, Master Shakespeare? Grandfather has some amazing ones."

The playwright nodded. "I need to do a Scottish play," he said, "if I'm going to keep our new Scottish king happy."

"But Grandmother served Anne Boleyn, Queen Elizabeth's mother!" Meg put in. "Aren't you going to tell *her* story?"

"I wouldn't dare!" laughed Master Shakespeare. "Would I show Anne Boleyn as a villain who deserved to die? The Queen would have me executed!"

"No! She was the victim of her monstrous husband, Henry!" Meg argued.

"Ah! So, you want me to show her as the innocent victim of a brutal king?"

"It's the truth."

"But that king was Queen Elizabeth's *father*! She'll *still* have me executed. No, Meg, if you don't mind, I'll tell Henry VIII's story when Elizabeth is long dead and buried."

"I was trying to tell Master Shakespeare about my family," I said.

"Don't let me stop you," smiled Meg.

"My *father*, Sir James Marsden, manages the estate and the mines and the collier ships that carry our coal to London. But he sailed with Sir Francis Drake around the world and against the Spanish Armada."

"He is also the most pompous magistrate you have ever met," Meg added.

"I used to think that, when I was younger. But now I see that he's shy and unhappy. He doesn't know how to show his feelings."

Master Shakespeare nodded wisely. He knew what I meant. He seemed to understand people better than anyone I had ever met.

"Will's mother, Lady Marsden, was a lady-in-waiting to Mary Queen of Scots. She could tell you wonderful stories about her execution. As bloody as *Titus Andronicus*!" Meg told him. "That would make a good story."

Again Master Shakespeare shook his head. "Mary was

King James's mother. If he saw her story on stage, he'd have me executed when he took over the English throne. It seems as if your family have marvellous tales, Will. But I'll never be able to tell them. It's too dangerous."

"Then the stories will be lost!" cried Meg.

"No. Someone else can tell the stories, maybe fifty years from now, when I'm long dead," he told her.

"Who?" she asked.

"It's young Will's job," he said.

"I want to be an actor, not a writer," I laughed.

"And so did I," Master Shakespeare said. "But I had stories that had to be told. I learned how to tell them. An actor's tale is soon forgotten, but a writer's stories can live for a thousand years. One day you'll find you have to put your family's stories down on paper, Will."

He was right, of course. He was the wisest man I ever met.

"The family tell stories every night after supper," Meg said. "Perhaps they'll ask you to tell one tonight."

"Then I'll tell them the story of my play, *Romeo and Juliet*," he offered.

"What's that?" Meg asked.

"The story of two lovers, Romeo and Juliet. Their families hated one another. So that they could escape together, Juliet took a drug that made her appear to be dead. When she'd been placed in her tomb, Romeo went to rescue her."

"No!" Meg laughed. "They have to be *true* stories,"

He stroked his beard. "In that case I'll tell them a story of spying and death. I'll tell them the story of Christopher Marlowe."

"Tell us now!" Meg demanded.

"Patience, Meg, patience!" Hugh said. "You'll hear it at the fireside in Marsden Hall."

"If we get there," Master Shakespeare said quietly.

We'd been in high spirits and death was hundreds of miles from our hearts until he spoke those words. "Why do you say that?" I asked.

"There are some woods ahead," he said nodding towards them.

"Bournmoor Woods," I told him. "Our family own them."

"A good place to hide and attack someone?"

"It has been done before," I said.

"Just the sort of place where Skeres or Frizer would lie in wait for us."

"They don't know we're here," I said.

"Someone does," murmured Master Shakespeare. "A man on horseback was sitting on the far hill, watching the road."

"That's Penshaw Hill," I said. "You can see all the roads along the River Wear from the top of that hill."

"He was looking this way. When he saw us he started off down the hill and headed this way. He'll travel much faster than we can. I guess we'll meet somewhere in the middle of your Bournmoor Woods – if he *wants* to meet us. It may be easier for him to sit behind a tree, wait for us to pass and shoot us in the back." Master Shakespeare reined back Romulus. "Should we take the chance?" he asked.

"No," I said, jumping to the ground. "I know the paths through the woods. I'll run round the river path and get behind him."

"I'll come with you," said Meg.

I knew better than to argue with her, or tell her that girls don't fight. Meg was as good in a desperate struggle as any boy. I smiled and said, "Thanks, Meg."

She grabbed a rope that we used to lash the stage boards together. "We may be able to trip his horse and take him alive," she said.

I ran to the edge of the woods, then took a track to the right that led down to the river. My days on the road and the effort of setting up and performing every night had kept me fit. I was scarcely panting as I turned again up the path from the river to the crossroads. We had come round in a half circle. We looked back along the road that Romulus and the cart would be travelling down.

In the dappled light that spilled through the trees I could see a figure clearly on the road. He was sitting on a horse and had his back turned towards us. It was cool in the shade of the ancient trees and he had his collar pulled up against the chill ... or perhaps, I thought, he was hiding his evil face. I grew angry. He was so sure of himself that he wasn't even bothering to hide behind a tree.

Meg picked up a stone the size of my fist and fastened the end of the rope tightly around it. She showed me quickly how the weighted end would wrap itself around a tree trunk when it was swung. "We used to use it to catch stray ponies," she said. "I'm still a good shot, but he'll duck if he sees me aiming to wrap this round his neck."

"What do you want me to do?"

"Walk down the left of the path while I walk down the right. When we get close enough I'll nod to you. Call out to him. As he turns towards you, I'll come behind, catch him round the throat with this and pull him off his horse. I'll use the rope to tie him up if you take his sword and dagger or pistols."

It was dangerous, especially if he had a loaded cross-bow under his dark-brown cloak. As he turned to me, he could loose off the bolt before Meg choked him. The closer I got, the less sure I was of the plan. I could see the cloak had a brown fur collar, just like my father's magistrate's cloak. That might protect him from Meg's rope and she might fail to pull him down.

Meg was moving lightly down her side of the path, stepping over twisted roots and round low bushes. The fallen leaves were damp and silent underfoot so we closed in on the man without him hearing a thing.

His gaze was fixed on the road back to Durham and he must have been wondering why the wagon was taking so long. From the corner of my eye I saw something flutter. Meg was waving a hand to attract my attention. She held up three fingers and mouthed the word, "Three."

I understood. She crouched, ready to spring. "Two!" she mimed.

The man finally shifted in his saddle and half turned towards me. The horror of recognizing him took my breath away. As Meg gave a nod and jumped up, I somehow found my voice. "No, Meg! No!"

The man's startled face looked at me. I rushed from the undergrowth and lunged towards Meg. She released the weighted end of the rope as I reached her. It hummed through the still air and there was a choking cry as it wrapped itself twice around the neck of the horseman.

I snatched at the rope, but only succeeded in hauling the man off his horse. He tumbled backwards and fell heavily into a bush. If he'd fallen on to the road he'd have broken his neck.

"Get the sword, Will!" Meg cried. "Don't just stand there like a moonstruck donkey!"

"But, Meg!" I gasped.

There was a rattle of wheels from the road as Hugh and Master Shakespeare whipped Romulus into a fast amble and hurried to help us. The only other noise was the gurgling noise of the horseman as he struggled to breathe. I tore the rope off his neck and Meg snatched it from me. She threw it over his head and began to loop it round his chest to fasten his arms to his side.

"No, Meg!" I moaned.

"Well done, you two!" Master Shakespeare cried, jumping down from the cart. He held a heavy, blunt sword from the props basket as if he planned to brain our captive. He stared at him. "But this isn't Nicholas Skeres," he said. "And it's not Ingram Frizer either! Tell us your name, you stuffed cloak-bag of guts!"

The man clutched at his throat, retching and gasping as he struggled to get his breath. "His name is Marsden," I said quietly. "Sir James Marsden."

Hugh Richmond stepped forward. "God's truth, young Will, it's your father!"

Meg gave a whimper like a kitten and her lips began to move in a hurried prayer.

My father's breath returned and his face turned quickly from white to deep purple. His eyes bulged and spittle was frothing on his lips as he struggled to find the words to match his outrage. "Thieves! Murderers! Cutthroat villains! I'll hang you all for this! You ... you ... you dare to attack the local magistrate."

"Sorry, Father," I said. "We didn't know it was you."

"That is beside the point!" he said, adjusting his rope-mangled collar and struggling to his feet. "You do not go attacking innocent horsemen on the public highway!"

"We thought you were out to kill us," Meg said quickly.

"Then you were right, Meg Lumley. I most certainly *am* out to kill you. In fact, if I could think of a way to kill you more slowly than hanging I would sentence you to that!"

"We're awfully sorry," Hugh said.

"Sorry, he says! Would you be saying sorry to Lady Marsden as you carried my corpse back to Marsden Hall? Would you? What good would your sorry be then?"

"There are killers after us, Father," I said.

He turned on me, his bottom teeth bared like a bulldog ready to bite. "I know that, you foolish boy! That's why I was on the road, waiting here to warn you!"

"You know?" Master Shakespeare said sharply. "How could you know?"

My father took a long breath through his thin nose. "I suppose you must be the famous William Shakespeare that my son admires so much."

"I am, sir, at your service."

"I have had a letter from your wife."

"Anne?"

"Yes, I do believe that is her name. She knew you were headed this way and sent a horseman ahead to warn us of the danger you face. We've been expecting you for a week." My father pulled a letter from his doublet and held it out to the playwright.

Master Shakespeare read it carefully, then repeated it to us.

My dearest William

I write to you with fearful news. Two days after you left for the north I was visited by the one-eyed man you call Skeres. It seems he searched the Evesham road and found no word that you had passed that way. Then he returned to Castle Bromwich and called on the Arden family. He told them that he had been sent with a message to our dear daughter, Judith. He said Judith had to return to Stratford with him as I was ill. As soon as he got her out of the house, he kidnapped her and has hidden her away. Of course, I knew he might be playing a trick and told him I did not believe him. He allowed me time to send a message to the Ardens and it seems it was true. Judith had left with a one-eyed man.

This Skeres then insisted that I tell him where you had gone, or he would send Judith back to me, one limb at a time. He could have threatened me with every kind of torture and I would never have told him where you were heading. But I cannot face the thought of Judith being harmed by these dreadful men. Forgive me, husband, but I told them you were making for Marsden Manor in Durham.

Judith has not been returned to the Ardens. I am sure Skeres and Frizer will hold her till they have dealt with you. But, if this letter to the Marsden family reaches you first, at least you have a chance to defend yourself. Judith does not even have that chance. What else could I do? What would you have done, my husband?

I have put your life at risk to save our daughter's life. They say they only wish to talk with you, but I do not believe the man. Save yourself, then return and save her.

Your loving wife, Anne

Master Shakespeare was trembling as he held the letter. "Threatening the child so the father will obey," he whispered.

"It's *Titus Andronicus*, isn't it?" I said.

He nodded slowly, his high forehead creased with worry. "And that ended in fearful bloodshed. When the avenger demands revenge, then no one wins. Everyone loses."

My father, for once in his life, seemed to sense someone else's suffering. "We must get you safely back to Marsden Manor first, sir," he said. "The village wise woman, Widow Atkinson, has a cottage nearby. Leave your theatre wagon behind her turf hut – it will be safe there. If this man Skeres is looking out for you, he'll be expecting you to arrive in that. I'll send a wood cart out into Bournmoor Woods to collect dead branches. You can hide under those and we'll bring you to safety in the hall."

The playwright was numb. His clever brown eyes were dull and empty. Even Hugh was drooping like a willow branch and Meg's small face was tight with pain.

"On the stage," she said quietly, "on the stage it seems an exciting game. But, when it happens to someone real – it's awful, Will."

I put an arm around her shoulders. "We'll find a way out. We always do."

"But not the *Titus Andronicus* way," she said as we led Romulus along the path to Widow Atkinson's cottage in the woods.

"Why not?" I said bitterly. "If we can kill Skeres and Frizer, then we can release Master Shakespeare's daughter."

She sighed heavily. "No, Will. Remember the play? Revenge brings more revenge. Skeres and Frizer have friends. If we kill them, then someone kills us and someone kills them and so it goes on. It's a circle. It goes round and round and only stops when there's no one left alive. We need to save Judith *and* break the circle."

I shook my head. "If you can find a way to do that, then you're cleverer than me."

For a moment there was the familiar spark in her eye. "I always have been, Will, I always have been!"

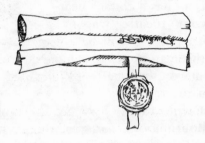

Chapter Ten

"Murder most foul"

MEG LUMLEY'S STORY

When I told Will I'd think of a way to save Judith Shakespeare, I didn't have a plan, you understand. But I'd said it, and I had to stick with it, or Will would never trust me again.

Sir James Marsden soon forgot my attack on him. He was too busy fussing and planning to bring his guests safely to his home. I kept quiet. He had not liked me when I first came to his magistrate's court as an orphan two years before. He'd wanted to put me in a workhouse, but his wife, Lady Marsden, had taken pity on me and brought me into Marsden Hall as a servant.

Lady Marsden had no daughters of her own, and she became fond of me. Within a year she had made me her own maid and taught me reading and numbers. It took Sir James a long time to accept me, even though I had proved my loyalty and my value to the house. I knew that one mistake could make him turn his anger against me again.

The first problem was to save ourselves, before we thought about saving Judith Shakespeare. We hid the wagon at Widow Atkinson's house and, one by one, made our way to Marsden Hall. Skeres and Frizer knew us all by sight, so we had to disguise ourselves. I borrowed a

shawl from my friend, the widow, and hobbled to the side entrance of the Hall as if I were a beggar.

By dinner time we had all gathered safely in the great hall of the old house. After the grease and gristle of tavern food it was good to have fine, fat duck in a rich, spiced sauce cooked by my friends in the kitchens.

As the church clock struck one in the afternoon, we gathered at the fireplace for a meeting to plan our next actions. But at Marsden Hall things never seem to work that way. Once the Marsdens gathered round the fire, they wanted to talk about the past and seemed to forget the dangers that the present held. After supper someone usually said, "I remember when ..." and a story began.

Now they had a guest – one of the world's greatest tellers of tales. The family were not going to miss the chance to learn a new story. Great-Uncle George, an ancient knight with a thick white beard, started the questioning.

"Our friend Hugh Richmond here has done noble work for his queen," he said. "Do you work for Her Majesty?"

Master Shakespeare smiled. "If you are asking me if I am a spy, then the answer is 'yes'."

"It's strange," said Grandmother, "that you are both actors and both spies."

Master Shakespeare looked at her silently for a moment

and then said softly, "I am talking to a family that loves Queen Elizabeth, aren't I?"

"Hah!" Grandmother cackled. "I knew the woman when she was a child. I never liked her very much. A hard and selfish little woman, just like her brute of a father. No, Master Shakespeare, we are loyal to England, not to some bald head that wears a golden crown."

The playwright nodded slowly. "Even better. I think many of us feel the same way. This household is loyal to England. So I can tell you secrets and know they will never be repeated outside this hall."

"Never doubt that!" Grandfather said stiffly.

"Since I met your grandson, Will, I never have," our guest said graciously. (I'll swear young Will blushed when he heard this and all eyes were turned towards him.) "So I will tell you some secrets of Secretary Cecil's spy system and, once you understand, you may be able to help me find a way out of my miserable situation."

"It must be hard to have a daughter threatened," Lady Marsden said quietly. She had no daughter, but she was looking at me and I felt a prick of tears at the back of my eyes.

Master Shakespeare bowed his head and began his story ...

MASTER SHAKESPEARE'S STORY

It began maybe thirty years ago with the Queen's late secretary, Sir Francis Walsingham. He was a cunning man with a sharp brain and a terrible hatred of Catholics. Sir Francis and the Queen decided that the best way to defeat an enemy was to know all his or her secrets. So they began to enlist the aid of spies.

They went to the universities at first to find bright young men who could travel to the Continent as gentlemen and report on enemy preparations. We knew about Philip's Spanish Armada plan before his ships were even built!

But here in England, we needed men who could travel the country and mix with men and women of all classes, men who would be at home with nobles and with peasants, but belong to neither and be loyal to Walsingham and the Queen.

Actors were the perfect spies. They were hired and protected by lords, yet travelled the country and mingled with the poorest. In my own Globe Theatre I look down and see the poorest scum of London standing as groundlings, then look up to the boxes to see the greatest lords of the land.

Actors can disguise themselves and pretend, of course. A spy is never what he seems. Actors listen to people in the towns and report back to the Secretary of State. Actors listen to lords and report back to the Secretary of State. If he places a spy or two in every acting company, the secretary can have a secret picture of England without ever leaving his office.

Walsingham decided to use actors as spies. Actors were his eyes and ears. Then he made an exciting discovery. He hired a brilliant young man called Christopher Marlowe – everyone called him "Kit" Marlowe. Kit didn't just act. Kit wrote plays. Kit wrote the most wonderful plays ever performed on the English stage! He wrote in poetry that was like music – he wrote about characters who came alive in front of your eyes – he wrote stories that made you laugh or cry or shudder with fear ... and sometimes all at once.

When I saw his play *Tamburlaine* I knew that I wanted to write plays like that. I sought out Marlowe to ask for his advice. After all, he'd been to university and learned all those skills – I'd only been to a school in Stratford.

I found Marlowe in one of his favourite places, one of the lowest, filthiest taverns in London. Playwrights aren't paid much – three or four pounds for a play – and spies are only paid when they produce some useful information. So Marlowe was always short of money. I know that, but I also believe that he went to those cheap taverns because he enjoyed the atmosphere. He loved the crime and filth and the very danger. Marlowe loved danger. Marlowe *was* danger.

I met him in a London alehouse, where the roof beams brushed your head and the horn windows let in as much light as a dungeon. He was the same age as me, but he seemed much older.

"I want to write plays like you, Master Marlowe," I said.

"Then do it."

"What?"

"Do it. Don't tell me about it. Don't talk about it. Don't *think* about it. Do it."

"Where do I start?"

"With a quill, a pot of ink and a sheet of paper," he said.

Kit Marlowe had a round, wide-eyed face and a fine

beard. He looked so young and lively, yet his heart was as old and cold as the River Thames itself. Those wide eyes were tiger-bright. Somehow that hard man wrote plays that would melt stones. I knew him for five years, yet never came close to understanding him.

When I had bought him enough to drink he became more mellow. I picked at his brains till I had enough clues and set off to write my first play, *Titus Andronicus*. My own company, the Lord Chamberlain's Men, bought it and it was a success. It was a crude piece, an excuse to shed blood and show endless murders on the stage, but it was popular. It's still one of my most popular plays.

The next time I met Marlowe he had changed towards me. He showed me more respect. "Tell me, Shakespeare," he said, "do you make a living from your writing and act-ing?"

I sighed. "I am an actor-sharer so I get some of the prof-its from the theatre. But I have a wife and three children back in Stratford. I can keep myself, but I wish I had more spare money to send to them."

He looked at me carefully and shifted on the inn bench so his mouth was close to my ear. "Would you like to make some more money?"

"Of course," I told him.

"Then you can work for Secretary Walsingham, the way I do."

"The Queen's secretary? What could I do for him?"

"A lot, my friend. A lot. If I take you to him, will you swear not to tell anyone of the meeting?"

"Yes," I said. I was uncertain, but excited at the thought of meeting someone so near to the Queen.

"Then follow me," he said.

We left the inn and walked through the crowded London streets till we came to some of the great houses on the Thames. Marlowe seemed to know every alley and path in that district. I was soon lost in the maze of high walls and sudden entrances, dark doorways and shuttered windows.

At last we came to a small oak door set in a brick wall and entered a quiet garden. In a hedge-sheltered seat facing the river Secretary Walsingham himself was sitting, reading some papers. He was a fearful man, dressed in black with a cream ruff and a paler face. His eyes were sunken and, in the shadows, his head looked like a skull.

For the next hour he questioned me to test my loyalty to England, the crown and the Protestant church. When he was satisfied, he said, "I use actors for my eyes and ears." He went on to explain how we could travel the country and report back to him on what people in the taverns and the castles, the marketplaces and the mansions, were saying about the Queen and her government.

"I understand."

"But men like you and Kit Marlowe here are different. I can use you as my mouth too."

"How?"

"You can write plays that carry messages we want the people to hear. You can show plays about kings like

Henry VI. Show what disasters happen when a monarch is over thrown. Turn the people against the Queen's enemies. Show them that it is better to support Elizabeth than Catholics, traitors and invaders."

It meant the government taking some control of my writing. "What would I gain by that?" I asked.

Walsingham leaned forward. "The support of the Queen herself. The protection of her government. You would be free to travel where you wanted with a royal licence. You could keep your playhouse open when the rest of the playhouses are closed by the magistrates. You would have such powerful friends no one would dare to close you down."

I was young and ambitious and the idea of so much power was attractive. In short, I agreed to spy for Walsingham and to write plays that would carry the message of loyalty to Elizabeth.

Marlowe introduced me to two men who would show me the codes and explain the system to me. "Meet your new colleagues," Kit Marlowe said. "Meet Nicholas Skeres and Ingram Frizer."

These men were no actors. They were the men on the other side of the spying trade. The assassins. I soon learned that if I reported a man for speaking out against the Queen, that man disappeared. Skeres and Frizer worked quickly and silently.

I became careful not to name men; naming someone meant a death sentence. But I went on writing my plays. The Queen was one of my greatest admirers. Fame and money were coming my way. Even Anne was happy in Stratford, seeing me every summer, and knowing she was storing up my wealth at home for the day I could afford to retire and be with our family for good.

When Walsingham died the crafty little Robert Cecil took over. My spying for Cecil changed very little, and it took up little of my time or energy, I must admit. Kit Marlowe and I became rivals in the popular theatre, but there was enough room in the theatres for both of us to live well. We were rivals, but never enemies.

Life was good, I was happy and it all seemed so harmless. Elizabeth had executed her cousin Mary Queen of Scots and Francis Drake had driven off the Armada. England seemed safe. But, of course, it was all an illusion – a dream, like one of my plays.

I discovered that when I met Kit Marlowe that last time. The last time ever. He came to my rooms at Holywell Street in Shoreditch. He worked much harder at his spying than I had ever done. He slept little and spent most of his time in the meanest taverns in London. It showed in his face. His skin had once been smooth and pale, now it was blotched and coarse.

It was early morning and he looked as if he hadn't been to bed. His eyes were red and sore and his clothes were dirty and carelessly thrown on.

"Are you well, Kit?" I asked him.

"Not as well as you, William Shakespeare," he spat.

"I'm sorry," I said.

"While you grow fat and rich, I am barely surviving. Do you know I was arrested for having Catholic books in my possession?"

"I'd heard," I said.

"It's not true! They were planted there!"

The world of spying was a world of lying and treachery. I could well believe that Marlowe had upset his masters and was being blamed for things he hadn't done. They could invent some crime and have him locked away.

"I'm sure you're innocent," I said.

He turned on me, his eyes wild. "This Cecil is the traitor!" he shouted.

I hurried to the door to make sure that no one had

heard that insane cry. Men had been executed for saying less than that. "Hush, Marlowe!" I said.

He lowered his voice, but spoke faster and more angrily. "The Queen is getting old. Cecil will survive her. He wants to choose the next monarch. He will support James VI of Scotland and James will reward Cecil when he takes the Queen's throne."

"Probably."

"But I am not one of Cecil's men. I was Walsingham's man. Cecil doesn't like me – nor does he like Skeres or Frizer," he said. "If James VI takes the English throne I will be murdered. Cecil will make sure of that."

"No, Kit!" I said.

"Yes, William," he hissed. "This criminal charge is just the start of it. He'll get me locked away and forgotten. Then, when the time is right, I'll be quietly done to death. Just like Henry VI in your play." Suddenly his creased face relaxed. "I saw it last week, William. A great play. You are becoming a better writer than me!"

"If you spent more time in the theatre and less on spying, you could write better," I suggested.

"It's too late," he said. "I'm in too deep. There's only one way out of this. I have to leave England now."

"And go where?"

"The Continent. Anywhere. I'm meeting with Skeres and Frizer today. We'll plan something. Then the London theatres will be all yours, my friend. After tomorrow, Kit Marlowe, the playwright, is dead. I only hope Kit Marlowe, the man, can survive."

I was shocked at the loss. Marlowe would be greater than me if he would only keep on writing.

I took his hand and grasped it. "I understand why you have to go … but you must come back one day – when the old Queen dies."

"If James VI is on the throne, and Cecil is his secretary,

Kit Marlowe can never come back. Good luck, William Shakespeare," he said. "The English theatre is all yours, my friend. I leave it in your good hands."

And he left. I was too shaken to do any writing that night.

When I arrived at the theatre the next morning for rehearsal, there was only one subject on every man's lips. The book-keeper took me to one side of the stage, his face like a tombstone. "It's Kit Marlowe, Master Shakespeare. He was at a tavern in Deptford last night. There was a fight. Marlowe was stabbed in the eye."

"Was he badly injured?" I asked.

"He was killed, Master Shakespeare. Killed."

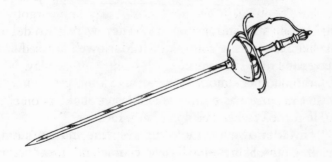

CHAPTER ELEVEN

"O, villain, villain, smiling damned villain"

WILL MARSDEN'S STORY

My family are strange people. They were shocked by Master Shakespeare's story of Kit Marlowe's death. At the same time they enjoyed it!

Grandmother's mouth was set in a thin, grim line. "It wasn't as simple as that, was it, Master Shakespeare?"

He turned to her. "Simple, Lady Eleanor?"

"This Marlowe was mixed up in spying and murdering. So are these Skeres and Frizer characters. This was no simple tavern fight, was it?"

The playwright smiled at her. "You have sharp wits."

"I have *old* wits," she cackled. "I know *people* and I have lived in a king's court where plots were thicker and darker than a seam of Durham coal. Men like Marlowe don't die in their beds and they don't die in accidents – unless somebody has arranged the accident very carefully."

Master Shakespeare bowed his head towards her. "It is true that Marlowe had displeased our master, Robert Cecil. It is possible that Cecil ordered Skeres and Frizer to kill him. But there was an inquest held. Skeres and Frizer were cleared and out of prison in a month."

"What was their story?" my father asked. His work as a magistrate was also one of his chief interests. He enjoyed listening to old crime stories and sitting in judgement on them all over again. The idea of an inquest was something he could understand.

"I wasn't there, you understand, but I have read the report. I can even recite it for you – I was interested in Marlowe's death at the time. That report stayed in my mind the way the lines of a play do with any actor." He rose to his feet and stood in the half-circle of listeners, his back to the low fire and repeated the report word for word:

"It happened that Christopher Marlowe met with a certain Ingram Frizer and Nicholas Skeres at a house in Deptford. They met at the tenth hour before noon on the thirtieth day of May in the thirty-fifth year of the reign of Queen Elizabeth. The room was in the house of a certain Eleanor Bull, widow. They passed the time together there and dined. After dinner they walked together quietly in the garden belonging to the house. At the sixth hour after noon they returned from the garden to the room and ate supper together there. After supper Ingram Frizer and Christopher Marlowe argued and exchanged angry words, since they could not agree about the payment of the sum of pence – the reckoning."

"I want to know what they were talking about from ten in the morning till six at night," my mother said in her quiet voice. "That's eight hours! I can imagine an argument building up over eight hours and ending in violence. If we knew what they were talking about, we'd know what happened."

"Exactly, Marion," my father nodded. "This story of a sudden row about the reckoning sounds most unlikely."

Master Shakespeare spread his hands. "No one ever asked what the talk was about. I'm sure it must have been about spying. Someone important warned the magistrate not to ask too many questions about that meeting."

"And the same important person made sure Frizer was pardoned," my father added.

"In that case, the whole inquest must have been a lie!" Grandfather said. "The whole report may be false – the argument about the reckoning. All we know for certain is that Marlowe died!"

"No!" I said excitedly. "We had a killing in Bournmoor Woods last year where even the victim wasn't who we thought he was."

That set off another babble of excited talking. "We know nothing," Master Shakespeare cried. "So anything is possible."

"But carry on, Master Shakespeare," my father said. "The magistrate may not have asked about their meeting. But he must have reported exactly how the death occurred."

The playwright plucked at his beard as he remembered where he had left off with the report.

"Christopher Marlowe was lying on the bed in the room where they had supped. He moved angrily against Ingram Frizer as they exchanged these angry words. Ingram Frizer was sitting in the room with his back towards the bed

where Christopher Marlowe was lying. He was sitting at the table with Nicholas Skeres. Christopher Marlowe suddenly drew Ingram Frizer's dagger which was at his back. With the same dagger Christopher Marlowe gave Ingram Frizer two wounds on the head to the length of two inches and a depth of one quarter inch. Ingram Frizer, in fear of being slain, struggled with Christopher Marlowe in self-defence. He tried to get the dagger back from him and it so happened that, in the struggle, he gave Christopher Marlowe a wound over his right eye to the depth of two inches and a width of one inch. From this wound the said Christopher Marlowe then and there instantly died."

The family had listened in silence. Now they all wanted to talk. Great-Uncle George had the loudest voice and he was heard first. "Nonsense!" he roared. "If Marlowe meant to kill Frizer he would stab him in the back. A ruffian like this Marlowe wouldn't have the whole of a man's defenceless back to aim at and only put a couple of scratches on his scalp! Why didn't the magistrate ask Frizer that?"

"I want to know why Frizer had his back turned," Grandfather put in. "If you are arguing with a man, you don't turn your back on him. Especially if that man is as violent as Marlowe seems to have been."

"And how did he get stabbed in the eye?" Grandmother asked. "He must have been attacking Frizer with the point of the knife. Frizer must have been a strong man to twist the knife all the way round in Marlowe's hand so that the point was turned upwards. Doesn't sound likely to me!"

She rose to her feet. "Lie on the table, Will!"

"Why?" I asked.

"Because you are Christopher Marlowe!" she snapped. "And that's your bed."

It was no use arguing with Grandmother in this mood. I lay on the table. She sat next to Grandfather at the fire-place and turned her back on me. "I'm Ingram Frizer and your grandfather is Nicholas Skeres. Now argue with me."

"Oh! Ah ... I'm not paying the bill!"

Grandmother turned slowly. Her face was pale with the thick white make-up she used. Her eyes were narrow. "Call yourself an actor?"

"No, I'm a playwright!"

"I'm talking to Will Marsden now, not Christopher Marlowe!" she creaked impatiently.

"Sorry," I said.

"That is the weakest acting I've ever seen. Try again! Pay your share of the bill, Marlowe!"

"Why should I?" I said fiercely. "I get paid little enough as it is. You called this meeting. You pay."

"You are a mean, penny-pinching little toad, Marlowe," she sneered.

I swung my legs off the table and drew my dagger. I stopped. "Why didn't Marlowe use his own dagger?" I asked suddenly.

"Good question," Grandfather nodded. "Carry on."

I put my dagger away and reached for Grandmother's belt where I snatched an imaginary dagger. She turned to face me and held up a hand. "Stop there, Will. All wrong! All wrong! You can stab my face from there. You could stab the hand that is reaching up to stop you. But I would *not* just sit there and let you stab me in the back of the

head. As soon as I felt you draw the dagger I would turn to defend myself!"

"Stab your face?" I cried. "That's a clue! The dead man was stabbed in the eye!"

"Hah!" my father cried. "So, Marlowe killed Frizer!"

"Then who went to prison for killing Marlowe?"

"Marlowe did! He took Frizer's place. Skeres *said* Frizer killed Marlowe. But Skeres could have been lying! Suppose Marlowe killed Frizer and took his place!"

"You knew Marlowe, Master Shakespeare," my father said. "Could this Frizer be the same man?"

"I've never seen Frizer," said Master Shakespeare.

"So, it's *possible*?" my father persisted the way he did when he was questioning suspects. "Marlowe killed Frizer and took his place."

"It's *possible*. It would let Marlowe escape from the trouble he was in over the Catholic books. But it's also possible that Frizer killed Marlowe," said Master Shakespeare.

"We've shown how unlikely it is," Grandmother argued.

Master Shakespeare turned to me. "Lie on the table again, Will."

I did as he said while he walked back to the fireplace and sat next to Grandmother. "I am Frizer. Skeres and I have waited all day for this moment. Marlowe is asleep on the bed – probably drunk too much wine. Marlowe has refused to do what we want. I stand up, walk across to the sleeping Marlowe and push my dagger into his eye. All the story about the argument was just a story they invented later. Skeres cut Frizer on the scalp to make the fight story look better."

Meg had been quiet while we had been exploring the story of Marlowe's "accident". When the talking died down she said, "None of this is helping to solve Master Shakespeare's problem of what to do about his daughter."

"That's true, Meg," my mother agreed.

"That is *not* true, Marion," my father said in his pompous way. He stuck out his bearded chin and went on, "The more we know about these two men the more we may discover their weaknesses. Nine years ago they murdered a man and got away with it. They have been protected by the Queen for all that time. Now the Queen is dying. Their shield is slipping away. They have to kill Master Shakespeare before a new king takes the throne."

Master Shakespeare shook his head. "I'm sorry, Sir James, but I don't understand why they are out to kill me!"

My father looked at me with some pride. "I think my son, Will, has solved the mystery."

I closed my eyes and thought about it. I knew that everyone in the room was looking at me and that didn't help me to think straight. "Kit Marlowe lived in the world of the theatre *and* the world of spies," I said. "Frizer and Skeres lived *only* in the world of spies. If I'm right, then Marlowe killed Frizer and took his place. Marlowe would then go and live in the world of spies where his secret was safe. He would *never* dare show himself in the world of the theatre again, or he'd be recognized. Master Shakespeare moves in both worlds – he could recognize Marlowe and the secret would be out. Marlowe would be tortured and questioned about the Catholic books and about the murder in Deptford. Master Shakespeare *has* to die," I said.

"Brilliant, Will," Meg said. "But this is *still* not solving the problem of Judith Shakespeare. If you are right, and she's a bait in the trap to catch her father, then they have him. As soon as Master Shakespeare shows himself, they will kill him."

"But Judith will live, if I give myself up to them," he sighed.

Meg moved close to him and squeezed his wrist. "Titus Andronicus sacrificed his hand to save his sons, and look what happened to him."

He nodded. "Tamora killed the sons anyway. You're right, Meg. If I give myself up, they may murder Judith anyway."

"What's the answer?" I asked.

For some reason everyone was turning to Meg to solve the problem. "Simple," she said. "We have to rescue Judith from Skeres and Frizer."

"Simple," Grandfather said softly.

"Do you know where she is being held?" Great-Uncle George asked. The idea of action rather than talk made his eyes bright.

"I'll find out," Meg said.

"How?" I wanted to know.

"One of those two men is in the Marsden area now," she said. "That's why they threatened Anne Shakespeare. To find out where her husband is."

"They are dangerous men, Meg," Master Shakespeare said. "We need more than a couple of actors and a few elderly gentlemen to tackle them."

Great-Uncle George drew in a deep breath, offended.

"Skeres and Frizer are experts, Great-Uncle," I said. "In a fair fight you would beat either of them, I know. But they would never meet you in a fair fight. They fight in the dark and stab in the back."

"But we have two great advantages," Meg said. "First, we are on our home soil. They won't get help from the beggars and street thieves the way they did in Stratford."

"And second?"

"Second? I'm sure that one will have stayed with Judith Shakespeare to guard her. I am certain there'll only be one of them in Durham."

"That makes it easier," Grandmother agreed. "I wish I was a fighting man like you, George," she sighed. "I'd soon deal with a villain like that. Taking a young woman prisoner – a gentleman would never do that."

"No," Meg said. "We have to take the man alive. We need to know where Judith is being held."

"Just what I was going to say," my father said. "First we find the villain. Then we capture him. Then we make him talk. Then we rescue Master Shakespeare's daughter. A clear simple plan. I like that!"

My grandmother snorted. "If it's that simple, my son, then tell us where to start!"

My father sniffed. "I have said, Mother, that first we find the villain."

"Off you go, then."

"What?"

"Find him."

My father glared at her. "It's not that simple."

"Sorry! I could have sworn you said it was," she said, and cackled.

"What do you suggest?" he said, irritated.

"Just one thing," she replied. "I suggest you listen to Meg Lumley. I suggest you listen ... and do exactly what she tells you."

CHAPTER TWELVE

"Would the night were come"

MEG LUMLEY'S STORY

I waited until it was dark. I slipped out of the warmth of the kitchens at Marsden Hall and into the damp mist of an autumn evening.

In towns like London and Stratford there is usually some light spilling through the windows of the houses. But when autumn mists covered the waning moon, Marsden Village was dark as a Durham mine. The villagers used tight wooden shutters to keep the cold out and the light in because they couldn't afford glass. And no one burned candles when they could eat and talk around the hearth by the light of their fires.

Master Shakespeare and the Marsden family had entrusted me with the task of finding Skeres. I told them I would look in the Black Bull Tavern in Marsden Village. Sir James had offered to send an armed guard with me. He *would* say that. He's a man, and men think that force is the best way to win a struggle.

Women know better. "If Skeres is warned of a troop of armed men, he'll escape," I said patiently. "He'll ride straight back to Stratford and put Judith Shakespeare to death."

"Well said, young Meg," old Lady Marsden crowed.

She had told them to leave me in charge. She said that out of mischief, and watched to see the men shuffle their feet and grumble.

"I'll go to the tavern and find out what I can. Once we know where he is, you can send the constable in to arrest him," I said.

"At least let me go with you," Will said.

"No, this is something I have to do alone. You're the magistrate's son. They don't hate you as much as they hate Sir James, but they still won't talk freely while you are there."

Will's young face folded into a hurt expression, but it had to be said. He thought I needed help, and he had the sort of kind heart that would always offer it – even when it wasn't needed.

The truth is I *did* need a little help, but not from the Marsdens. I headed for the cottage of old Widow Atkinson, just off the road through Bournmoor Woods. Even the stars didn't light this path, but I knew it well and soon found the way between the trees.

She was standing at the door when I arrived as if she expected me. Some villagers called her witch. Most of us knew her as the village wise woman. We never asked questions about where her wisdom came from, but I knew it wasn't from the Devil.

"I've come for a few costumes from the wagon," I told her. It was true. I didn't want to walk into the Black Bull and find Skeres looking at me. He'd be back on the road to Stratford before I could run home to Marsden Hall. I needed a disguise.

"You need a little more than that, Meg Lumley," she said. "Find your costume and then come in. We'll have a little word or two before you go."

She lent me a lantern to search the cart and I soon found the old cloak we'd bought from the farmers at Stratford.

We'd never use it on stage – audiences came to see riches not rags – but I'd known that I would need this again.

I found my way back to the door of the cottage. It glowed with a warm amber light from the peat fire and there was a dizzying scent of herbs and the perfumes of flowers. Some bundles were hanging over the fire to dry and others were spread on the rough oak table at the side of the door. There was only one room in the cottage and the widow's straw mattress lay at one end with sheepskin rugs for a quilt. It was warmer and more comfortable than all the grand and draughty rooms of Marsden Hall.

Widow Atkinson wasted no time with chat. "You'll not get Michael the Taverner to talk, you know. A year ago, perhaps. But now he knows you're one of the Marsden family, he'll shut tighter than a frog's mouth."

"So what should I do?"

She smiled. Widow Atkinson was as old as Will's grandmother, but without the white lead paste on her face, her skin was smooth and glowing like a woman half her age. "Threaten him, of course."

I liked the idea. "What with?"

"Last week, ten wagons of Marsden Manor corn went to the mill on the Wear. The miller ground it and sent it back, but there was a sack missing from every wagon that returned. Sir James was furious. He blamed the miller, of course."

"Of course!" I laughed. It's well known that millers are the biggest thieves in the world. No matter how much corn you send them, they always steal a bowl or two for themselves.

"But the miller hadn't stolen them. I have heard that a search below the floor of Michael Taverner's cellar might uncover some nice fresh flour!"

"That's interesting," I nodded.

"And Wat Grey is having a little trouble selling a black pony. It's lame and he has to hold on to it until it's fit."

"So?"

"So ... ask the steward of Lord Birtley's house to look at the pony. He may just say it is the young lady's animal."

I frowned. "Wat doesn't usually steal horses from so close to home."

"He thought he had a buyer in Lanchester ready to take it. If it hadn't been lame, it would have been over the hill by now. But he's stuck with a stolen pony and he could hang for it ... if somebody mentioned it to Sir James Marsden."

"Mistress Atkinson, you're wonderful!" I cried.

"Aye, but what you're doing is dangerous, Meg Lumley."

"No one else can do it. And a girl's life depends on my succeeding," I said.

"I know," she said. "That's the only reason I'm letting you go off on this madcap adventure." She reached under the table and pulled out a small drawer. She held out a pebble. It had been worn smooth and there was a hole clear through the middle. "Take this for luck."

"What is it?" I asked.

"An elf-cup," she said. "It's a powerful charm against the evil you're going to face."

I wrapped my hand around it. Maybe it had some magic, or maybe I just imagined it. But I felt safe when I held it. "Thanks, Mistress Atkinson," I said.

She sighed. "I wish I could do more to help you."

I slipped out of the door and into the damp air. I was soon walking back past the high wall of Marsden Hall and towards the village. I could smell the tavern before I reached it: the ale fumes that had seeped into the old timbers, and the stale food trampled into the rushes on the floor.

I opened the door carefully and looked in. There was no one-eyed man in the crowded taproom as far as I could see. I pulled the cloak around my neck, just to be sure, and stepped inside.

"Meg!" Michael Taverner cried, as soon as he saw me. His fat, unwashed face was running with sweat as it usually was in the hot, airless room. "Come to give me a hand?"

I knew I wouldn't be able to talk to him while he was so busy. I threw my cloak beneath a bench, rolled up my sleeves and began taking orders, collecting empty mugs and serving foaming full ones. At last the customers were all served and Michael wiped his hands on an apron so filthy it was hard to tell what colour it had originally been.

"You're the best worker I ever had," Michael grinned. In the weeks I'd been away he'd lost another green tooth until now there were more gaps than teeth. "Are you back to stay?"

I pulled him to one side. "I'm looking for a man," I said.

"Yes, it's about time you were married, young Meg. But I thought you had your sights set on Magistrate Marsden's son!"

The smoky light from the tallow candles was dim and it hid my furious blushes. "I mean, I'm looking for a villain."

He smiled broadly. "Ah! Sensible girl! You want to marry me, then!"

"Michael!" I cried. "I am looking for a man from London. He's an assassin and I have to find him before he kills the daughter of a friend."

He looked disappointed. "No villains in here," he said.

"I wouldn't let them stay in a respectable tavern like this."

"Ah!" I gasped. "It's not Taverner Michael I'm talking to! It's *Saint* Michael. I'll swear those are wings sprouting from your back and a halo glowing over your head."

He wiped his shapeless nose on the back of his sleeve. "I'm an honest man," he said, lifting a mug of ale to his blubbery lips.

"Honest men don't keep ten sacks of stolen flour under the floorboards of their cellars," I said.

"God's nails!" he gasped, and almost choked on the ale that found its way into his nostrils.

"Shall we ask Constable Smith to have a look?"

His red-rimmed eyes burned fiercely. "I'm looking after them for a friend," he said.

"That's all right then. I won't mention anything to Constable Smith."

"You're still one of us, Meg," he muttered.

"Yes, Michael. You're an honest villain. You wouldn't cut the throat of an innocent girl just to take revenge on her father," I said.

"Even I wouldn't stoop that low," he said and, for once, I believed him.

"The man I'm looking for would. And he *will* if I don't stop him."

"What's his name?"

"Skeres. Nicholas Skeres."

He shook his head slowly. "No one here of that name."

"He could be travelling under a false name. You wouldn't check his papers anyway."

"So what does he look like?"

"He's about thirty-five and he has only one eye," I said.

"No," he said again. "The only stranger I have here is a man called Frizer. Ingram Frizer."

I felt a sudden shudder of fear and excitement. "That'll be him!" I said. For some reason we'd been expecting Skeres – he was clearly the leader. But Skeres could well be guarding Judith Shakespeare. Skeres was the man who'd tried to kill Will in the Hanged Man and he would cut Judith's throat without a second thought. "Where is this Frizer now?"

"In his room. The best room with the four-poster bed, on the top floor."

"I know it," I said. "There's no way out except the door into the passageway, is there?"

"The window's too high to drop down," he said.

"Then guard the door while I fetch Constable Smith," I said.

The taverner looked unhappy at the thought of a guest being arrested, but he gathered the horse thief, Wat Grey, and a few of his most evil companions around him for a secret conference.

I ran through the village to the blacksmith's forge and rattled on the door that led to the rooms above. "Robyn Blacksmith!" I called. "Constable Smith!"

After a minute the shutter of the window above opened. In the light of his own lantern I could see his square face framed by the wiry hair and grizzled beard. "It's Meg Lumley, isn't it? Wait a moment and I'll be down."

It took me five minutes to explain the position to him. He armed himself with his sword and followed me to the Black Bull.

The little man who waited by the door for us was skeleton-thin and bone-white: Wat Grey, the local horse dealer. "He's still in his room, Meg," he said. "I've been keeping an eye on him."

I slapped his arm. "Thanks, Wat," I said. "No one has a sharper eye than you. Why, I'll bet you could see a lame black pony in the dark!"

"What!" he squawked.

"Nothing, Wat!" I said innocently. "But I'd like you to call him from his room so he doesn't know the constable is there, otherwise Frizer will come out armed and fighting."

He rubbed his skinny hands together and gave a twisted smile. "Yes, Meg, if that's what you want."

Widow Atkinson's information was proving useful. Still, I clutched at the elf-cup in my pocket and prayed. I waited in the taproom while Wat went with the taverner and the constable up to Frizer's room. The corridors were too narrow to clutter them with an audience, so I stayed behind.

A few minutes later there was a clatter behind the door. It crashed open and Ingram Frizer was carried into the room. Robyn the Smith had his huge arms wrapped round Frizer's body, pinning the spy's arms to his sides. Frizer's

pale eyes were staring and his face was as wooden as ever, but his legs were flailing and kicking at the air. He upset two or three tables as the constable carried him through the taproom and out of the door.

With a swift movement Constable Smith unfastened his belt and wrapped it round Frizer's chest. Then he turned him round, gripped his throat in a hand like a bear's paw and said, "Now, sir, I am arresting you."

"For what?"

"You'll see. Now, I can fasten your legs together, but then you wouldn't be able to walk to the Hall. In that case I'd have to grab you by the feet and drag you. Or I can leave your legs free and you can walk. Which would you prefer?"

"I'll walk," Frizer said. "I am innocent. You have no right to imprison me like this. It's against the law."

"Which law is that, sir?" the constable asked, as he spun his prisoner round, grasped the belt at his back and opened the outside door with Frizer's face.

"The law of England."

He was bundled, stumbling and slipping, along the road to Marsden Hall where Sir James was waiting, seated behind a table. Will sat to his right with pen and parchment ready to make notes. Hugh Richmond and William Shakespeare were not there, but the family sat

by the fire to watch.

Frizer repeated his objections to Sir James. "I demand justice in the name of the laws of England."

"Ah, but you're not in England now, you're in Marsden Manor now," Sir James Marsden said sternly. "I am magistrate here. I make my own laws."

"You can't do that."

"I can and I *do*," Sir James said. His son, Will, kept his head lowered, but I knew he was trying to hide a smile. Sir James Marsden was doing something I never thought he could. He was playing a part like an actor on stage in a tavern courtyard.

"You have kidnapped the daughter of a playwright named William Shakespeare."

"I haven't," Frizer said. He was calm now and ready to play Sir James at his own game.

"We have a letter from Mistress Shakespeare herself. She says she was threatened by a one-eyed man named Skeres."

"I have two eyes, Magistrate, and my name is not Skeres, it is Frizer."

For a moment Sir James was uncertain. "But you know this Skeres."

"I have met him."

"And you helped him kidnap Judith Shakespeare."

"Does your letter say that?" he asked.

Again Sir James hesitated. Will looked up, anxious now, not smiling. "No ... but ..."

"Then you have no evidence. You have to let me go!" Frizer gloated.

"You deny kidnapping Judith Shakespeare?"

"Of course."

"But you tried to kill me!" Will interrupted.

"No, I didn't," Frizer shrugged.

"In the Hanged Man!"

"That was Skeres, wasn't it?" the spy said, turning the question back on Will.

"Yes, but you were there."

"Did I raise a finger or a knife against you?"

"No ... but ..."

"Then you have to let me go!"

There was silence in the room. Sir James Marsden cleared his throat. "Constable Smith, take this man to the cellar below the kitchen. Put him in with a lantern and a flagon of water. We will question him again tomorrow."

"Yes, Sir James," the constable said and led the spy away. Frizer's face was as lifeless as a corpse, yet I'll swear that he had a faintly smug expression as he left the room.

Of course Will Marsden and his father turned and looked at me. "First we find the villain, then we capture him, then we make him talk," Sir James said bitterly. "It seems this last part of the plan is not going to be quite as simple as you made it sound, Meg Lumley. This is a ruthless and experienced villain. My mother suggested we leave the planning to you. So? What do we do now? Do you know how we can make this Ingram Frizer talk?"

I could not look him in his small, gloating eyes. I lowered my head, close to defeat. "No, Sir James, I don't."

CHAPTER THIRTEEN

"I must be cruel only to be kind"

WILL MARSDEN'S STORY

I felt Meg's shame as deeply as she did. It wasn't fair to expect Meg to do *everything*. She was the only one who believed she could. I knew then it was time I did something to help Master Shakespeare and his daughter.

"I know what we can do," I said.

Meg looked up at me, uncertain. "Frizer is trained as a spy," she said. "Walsingham must have trained him to expect this. If he's captured, he knows he mustn't talk"

"Even under torture?" I asked.

"Pah!" my father exploded. "The trouble is he knows that even a northern magistrate doesn't put suspects to the torture. I can duck witches in the river until they talk and I can lock criminals away for a day, but I can't use torture. He must be clinging to that hope."

"Who could stop you?" I asked.

"The law!" my father snapped. "The people in this area know I'm strict, but I always work to the letter of the law. If they see me breaking the law, then they will also feel free to break laws. No, I cannot use torture on Ingram Frizer and he must suspect that."

"Besides," Meg put in, "Frizer's friends might just take over the country when the Queen dies. Then Frizer will make sure they take revenge on Marsden Manor. They would destroy Sir James and all the family. It would be just like the play – revenge and more revenge."

"Just like the play!" I muttered, half to myself. "Just like *Titus Andronicus*." I turned to my father. "How long can we hold Frizer without a trial?"

"Until tomorrow tonight," he said.

"Then we have a day to prepare for his trial. With Master Shakespeare's help we should be able to do it. But we'll need the rest of the village to help us too."

"They hate me," my father said.

"But not so much as they hate a bully who kidnaps helpless women," Meg said. "I can make sure Michael Taverner and Wat Grey help. They will persuade the others. What do you want them to do?"

"Act out a bad dream. A nightmare in fact. You'll see!"

The idea excited me and, when I'd explained it, Meg was excited too. My father was not so certain, but then he hadn't seen the audiences when we'd been on tour.

I spent the next day in a fever of preparation. I needed everyone to know their part. For those who could read, I wrote a script – the first script I'd ever written. Even Master Shakespeare admired it.

Hugh Richmond took the people who couldn't read and showed them what to do. Meg used her popularity in the village to make sure everyone would join in, while my father organized the preparation of the courtyard at the back of the Black Bull.

By late afternoon the courtyard had been swept and swilled with water till the cobbles shone. A scaffold had been built on ale barrels like a stage for a play. The props were ready on the stage.

Benches were arranged in the yard for the older people

to sit and watch the action while the blacksmith made new iron brackets to take twenty torches. We decided that nightfall would be the best time for what we planned.

As evening fell we had a quick rehearsal for my first production, "The trail and execution of Ingram Frizer."

The production began with a parade, as so many plays do. Robyn Smith, the constable, opened the door to the cellar and brought Ingram Frizer out. He had not been given food so that his spirits would be low. "You've come to set me free, constable?" he asked.

"No, Frizer, I've come to take you to trial."

"The magistrate got nothing from me last night and he'll get nothing from me tonight. He'll have to let me go."

"We'll see what the witnesses have to say," Robyn Smith said and refused to answer any more questions.

Michael Taverner and Wat Grey were waiting at the gate to Marsden Hall. They were chained together by the legs. Constable Smith chained Frizer to little Wat Grey and began to lead them down the road to the tavern.

Some of the Marsden servants carried torches to light the way. They glowed like corpse candles in the misty air. A few villagers lined the roadside and began to follow the prisoners till a small procession formed. I walked behind the main actors.

"This is all your fault, Frizer," Michael Taverner hissed at the spy.

"Yes! Bringing trouble to our village," Wat Grey agreed.

"Shut up, you mewling kittens," Frizer spat, as he shuffled and tried to keep in step with Wat.

"Kidnapping is a hanging offence!" the taverner cried. "We are accused of helping you! We could dangle alongside you!"

"Only if they can find a rope long enough to go around your fat neck," Frizer sneered. "Don't worry. Magistrate

Marsden may threaten, but he would never dare to harm you. He doesn't scare me!"

"He scares me!" Wat wailed. "You don't know what he's like when he doesn't get his own way."

"Look!" Frizer replied angrily, hauling on the chain and forcing Wat to his knees for a few painful moments. "You are innocent of helping me."

"Ah, but that's where Magistrate Marsden is so dangerous! If he doesn't hang us for helping you, he'll hang us for some other crime he's invented. He can pay witnesses to say we've stolen something. *You* know we're being hanged for giving you shelter – but the court records will say we were hanged for thieving. It makes no difference to us! Either way we'll be dead!"

For the first time Frizer looked a little uncertain. The crowd was growing larger now and some were starting to mutter threats against the prisoners. "I've been in worse positions than this and survived," he said.

The group arrived at the Black Bull and were led by the constable into the courtyard. It was a brilliant and shocking stage for the theatre we were going to perform. The smoking torches turned every face red. The scaffold was hung in black and a gallows tree rose up till the top was almost lost in the mist. But the rope glowed orange and looked almost alive.

My father, Grandfather and Great-Uncle George were dressed in black robes with white collars to frame their serious faces. The crowd jostled and packed into the cobbled space. The mood was tense but excited, as it was at the start of a play – or before a public execution.

The three accused men were led on to the scaffold and fastened to a low rail to the left of their three judges. They looked across the stage to the gallows and to the silent figure who stood below them. I knew it was Master Shakespeare, yet that black hood with just three holes for his eyes and mouth made him look as sinister as the devil himself.

The crowd began to boo the prisoners and shake angry fists. Michael Taverner bared his gums and rotten teeth at them. Wat Grey simply looked terrified. Frizer's face was as blank as ever. Only the eyes moved a little more than usual, taking in the nightmare scene.

"Michael Taverner!" my father boomed in a voice like doom.

"What?" the owner of the Black Bull asked defiantly.

"I would advise you to show respect for this court, Taverner."

The fat man spat on to the stage and the crowd booed loudly. "Taverner, you are charged that you have helped one Ingram Frizer, a traitor and kidnapper. As such you are liable to be hanged if you do not answer my questions."

"You don't frighten me, Magistrate Marsden!" the taverner shouted.

My father straightened his shoulders and simply pointed to the hooded executioner. The disguised playwright crossed the stage while Constable Smith unfastened the taverner's shackles. Michael was dragged to the table where the magistrates sat and his hand was placed on the table. Master Shakespeare took out a knife that was the size of a small sword. It glinted red-gold in the torchlight and the crowd suddenly went silent.

"Has Frizer told you where he is keeping Judith Shakespeare prisoner?"

"No!" Michael said. Now his voice was hoarse with fear.

"You are lying."

"I'm not, Sir James, I'm not!"

"In that case you are also charged with selling watered ale below the strength the law demands. You have been found guilty in your absence."

"What?"

"I hereby sentence you to have your right hand cut off," my father said calmly as the executioner raised the butcher's knife.

"No!" Michael screamed.

"Have you suddenly remembered where Judith Shakespeare is hidden?"

"I don't know! I honestly don't know! On my life!"

Father looked at Grandfather and Great-Uncle George. They gave a single nod each. My father nodded at Master Shakespeare and the knife fell.

Michael Taverner's scream pierced the fog and disturbed the crows in Bournmoor Woods. The hand leapt across the scaffold, the crowd gasped and blood spurted over the table. Michael appeared to have passed out. "Dip that wrist stump in tar," my father ordered the constable lazily. "We don't want him to bleed to death."

The taverner's heavy body was dragged over the stage and out of sight.

Wat Grey was led forward next. He wore a thin shirt that had once been brown, but was stained black in places as if he suffered from the plague. The shirt was so thin that he was shivering in the cool night air.

"Sir James ... your honours ... I know nothing, nothing at all! This Frizer is a stranger. I only met him three days ago."

"You spoke to him?" Great-Uncle George asked.

"Yes ... but ..."

"And he never told you why he was here?"

"To meet some writer of plays. He had some business with this Shake-sword man."

"And you never asked what the business was?"

"No, your honour, sir."

"I find that hard to believe."

My father leaned forward. "So you refuse to tell us where Judith Shakespeare is being held?"

"I *would* tell you if I knew," Wat moaned.

My father shrugged. "Never mind. You are a notorious horse thief. This manor will be better off without you. You have been found guilty of the theft of a white stallion three weeks ago, and I hereby sentence you to hang."

"You can't do that!" the little man screamed.

"I just have," my father said, and he almost smiled.

"I mean – I mean you can't do that because my father was Lord Durham himself. I was an unwanted child and left to die in the gutters of Durham City. I was rescued by a tanner's wife and brought up as her own son!"

"Your tragic tale is no concern of this court," Grandfather told him.

"But it *is*, sir! Only a common man would hang. As the son of a lord I demand the honour of being executed by being beheaded."

The three magistrates put their heads together and discussed this for a long while. All the time the excitement in the audience was growing. From my position behind Frizer I could hear the villagers talking. I don't know what effect their words had on Frizer, but they terrified me.

"I've seen a dozen hangings," the village carpenter said, "but I've never seen anyone beheaded!"

"They say the lips go on moving for ten minutes after the head's cut off," his wife said.

"Get away!"

"That's what happened with Anne Boleyn."

"But the executioner made a bad job of Mary Queen of Scots. Three chops it took."

"Three chops and a bit of sawing," another villager put in.

Frizer stayed as still as the gallows pole. Finally my father looked up. "Very well, Wat Grey, your request is granted. There's a wood-chopping block in the corner of the yard. Just use that, Master Executioner."

The playwright gave a low bow of the head and led Wat off the scaffold and around the back. If Frizer had known what to look for he might have noticed that the man who emerged from the far side of the scaffold was much taller than the one who'd just left the platform. But it was shadowy in that corner and no one would recognize Hugh Richmond under the wig of greasy grey hair on the false head.

The crowd went silent. The suspense dragged on as the victim put his hands together and prayed for a minute. Finally the executioner placed the man's neck on the block while the constable held him down. In fact Robyn Smith's broad back stopped anyone getting a clear view as the man in the black hood hacked and hewed with his large knife.

The gasp from the audience was as great as any we had had on tour when we beheaded a character in *Titus Andronicus*. The cheer that went up made the torch flames flicker as the executioner held the dripping head aloft.

The head and body were removed while my father turned to the last prisoner. "Now, Ingram Frizer, a letter from Mistress Anne Shakespeare says that your friend, Nicholas Skeres, has kidnapped her daughter, Judith. Would you like to tell us where the girl is being held?"

Frizer was frozen like the village pond in winter. He stared like a sleepwalker. His mouth opened, but no sound came out.

"Speak up, man!" my grandfather shouted. "We old ones are a little deaf."

"Hanged Man," Frizer croaked.

"No! He was beheaded!" Great-Uncle George snapped.

"Hanged Man Tavern. Near Stratford. Hanged Man. Hay loft. Over the stables," he stammered.

The prisoner's knees were buckling and only the chains

seemed to be holding him upright. My father gave a grim smile. "Thank you, Frizer. Now why couldn't you have said that last night?" He dipped a finger in the pig's blood that covered the table. "It would have saved someone having to clear up all this mess!"

"What?" Frizer said in disbelief.

"The mess, man. It'll mean a few trips to the pump with buckets for some poor servant. Have you no thought for the servants?"

Frizer shook his dazed head.

"I am sending you on a ship to London with a copy of my report for Sir Robert Cecil. You will be held in the Tower of London while he decides your fate. Constable Smith – take this man to Wearmouth port and hand him over to the care of Captain Walsh. The captain knows what to do with him."

"Yes, sir," the constable said, as he unfastened the shackles and led the spy away. The villagers jeered him and pelted him with mud as he made his way through the crowd. Constable Smith did little to protect his prisoner.

The crowd watched Frizer being loaded on to a cart and led along the road to Wearmouth. When he was safely out of sight the villagers gave a great cheer and turned to the stage where the players were already gathering to take their bow. Hugh Richmond pushed his head through the blood-soaked collar of his shirt and laughed aloud, while Wat Grey shook hands with the people around the stage. Michael Taverner waved the severed hand at the crowd and invited everyone into the tavern for pots of ale.

My father, Great-Uncle George and Grandfather shook hands after a job well done and joked with the villagers. "You should become an actor, Sir James!" the carpenter called.

"One in the family is enough," my father told him sternly. Then he seemed to relax. "But I do think I played my part rather well. You can see where my son's acting ability comes from."

"But actors get paid, Sir James," Michael Taverner said slyly. "Are you going to pay me and Wat?"

"Yes!" my father said with a spark of joy in his eyes. "I am going to pay you ten sacks of flour."

The taverner's smile faded.

"Sacks of flour?"

"The ones beneath the floor in your cellar. You can *keep* them ... and I will just forget that I know they are there," he said quietly.

My father walked off the stage and the taverner muttered some vicious remarks about him, but he was dragged inside his tavern to serve ale to the excited crowd.

"That was a wonderful script you wrote, young Will," Hugh said. "Even *Titus* didn't get an audience as excited as that!"

"Thanks, Hugh," I said.

Only Meg and Master Shakespeare stood quietly outside the celebrations. They alone remembered that our task was just half completed. The most dangerous part was yet to come.

CHAPTER FOURTEEN

"The grave shall have a living monument"

MEG LUMLEY'S STORY

The morning after Frizer's trial we gave the strangest performance of *Titus Andronicus* that the world will ever see. Sir James gave his workers a half-day holiday and we agreed to perform our plays as we'd done on tour.

The audience were in a holiday mood in the courtyard of the Black Bull Tavern where the stage was still in place. But while other audiences had gasped in terror at the torture scenes, the Marsden villagers roared with laughter. They remembered the stage tricks we'd used the night before. When the head of Titus was carried on, it was the dummy head of Wat Grey that we used. No one laughed louder than Wat himself.

Will's scheme had worked wonderfully when mine had failed. I was proud of him, although, of course, I couldn't tell him that.

We all met for dinner at Marsden Hall after the performance. Lady Marsden insisted that now I should sit at the table with the family and not serve them as a maid. Will's grandmother secretly looked pleased and even Sir James didn't object. He was too busy playing his favourite role – master of Marsden Manor.

"These are dangerous times, Master
Shakespeare," he said. "I must admit I used
to think plays and players were a waste of
time. But watching your *Richard II* this
morning I could see how you are bringing
your message to the people. We must have a
peaceful handover of Queen Elizabeth's
power, or we'll face terrible times."

"Not my message, Sir James," the playwright said. "It's Secretary Cecil who
wants the English people to accept the
Scottish king."

"What does old Elizabeth want?"
Grandmother asked.

Master Shakespeare sighed. "I think
she would like to see riot and destruction when she dies.
That's why she's still using people like Skeres and Frizer.
It's simple spite. When she dies, she wants thousands of
others to die with her. She'd be happy to think that
England will tear itself apart without her."

We ate silently for a while. "But she's still alive," I said.
"She can have Frizer released from the Tower of London
as soon as your ship delivers him there. He could even be
back in Stratford with Skeres before we get there!"

Sir James took a deep breath and puffed out his chest
like a pigeon. "It just so happens that my ship *wasn't*
headed for London. That was a little deception I played
on our friend Ingram Frizer. This week the ship is going
across to France with a load of coal. Ingram Frizer will be
delivered to the mayor of Caen with a letter explaining
what he has been up to – especially his part in the death
of Mary Queen of Scots."

Slowly the joke spread round the table. "France has
just returned to the Catholic faith," Great-Uncle George

chuckled. "They'll enjoy having one of Elizabeth's spies for company."

Grandfather nodded. "They'll enjoy it so *much* that they may lock him in some deep dungeon so he'll *never* leave them!"

"But Skeres is still free," I reminded them.

The laughter died in the throats of the family. "Aye, Skeres," Hugh said. "He seems to be the dangerous one."

Master Shakespeare looked grim. "And he has my daughter. As long as Skeres is free, the Queen can spread her wickedness like a plague."

"There are three of us against a one-eyed man," Will Marsden said.

"Four of you," his mother said quietly. I could have kissed her.

"Four of us," Will agreed, glancing at me.

"Against one skilled assassin," Grandfather warned. "I wish I could go with you."

"Marsden Manor could send some armed men to help," Sir James offered.

"As soon as Skeres saw them, he'd cut Judith's throat,"

Master Shakespeare said. "We can't hope to defeat violence with violence. We have to defeat it with cunning."

His large, brown eyes were troubled. I turned to him. "We need to get back to Stratford, don't we? All the planning in the world won't rescue Judith while we sit here."

"You're right, Meg. We can plan when we get there and see what Skeres has done with Judith."

"We'll travel faster without the play wagon" I said.

"I know."

We left the dinner table and began preparing to leave that afternoon. Sir James promised to send the wagon with the props and costumes to the Globe, the next time a coal ship headed for London. Master Shakespeare used some of the profits from the journey to buy five horses for us – Romulus would be too slow. He too would travel to London on the coal ship.

We would ride four good horses and use the fifth for baggage and as a spare. Wat Grey found us the best horses in the district at a fair price.

"That must have been the first honest act of your life."

He scowled. "I'm sure I did another one ... once."

"When?"

"I can't remember."

"But this one made you feel good, Wat, didn't it?"

His face cleared. "It did, Miss Meg. I enjoyed helping that Master Shakespeare."

"Then perhaps you'll make a habit out of being honest," I said, as I led my horse away. When I looked back, the little horse thief was scratching his head as if he was thinking about it.

That afternoon we rode south, as far as the Scotch Corner on the London road. Here the road forked. The road to the west of Scotland joined ours down the east coast. The tavern at the fork was a gathering place for travellers. All the talk was about the dying Queen and her successor.

"You know that this sort of talk is banned in the Queen's own court at Richmond Palace?" Master Shakespeare said.

As the evening wore on, and the travellers had more to drink, the arguments in the taproom became more bitter and ugly. A farmer from Lancashire was a Catholic who wanted James VI of Scotland to take the English throne because James might have more pity for the Catholics. There was a sheep farmer who had suffered so many raids from Scotland that he said he'd rather have the devil than a Scotsman on the throne. And there was a soldier who said England had been peaceful for too long. He was looking forward to the battles that lay ahead.

"You see?" the playwright sighed, as we went up the narrow stairs to our beds. "England is tearing herself apart. Three Englishmen fighting with one another when they should be standing together. And it's all because Elizabeth won't name the person who'll take her throne."

The noise of the arguments downstairs went on for some hours and I slept badly.

The weather changed the next day and icy rain from the north drove against our backs. The road turned to

mud and we were glad we weren't driving the play wagon. Night fell early and it was already dark when we reached Doncaster, mud-stained and weary. The city guards were suspicious and read our passports carefully. "Where are you acting?" the sergeant of the guard demanded. "And where are your costumes?"

"We're on our way back to London," Master Shakespeare said. It was a small lie, but there was no need to tell the man the full story.

"Then make sure you're off the roads before dark tomorrow night. These are unsafe times, Master Actor," he warned us. "There are troublemakers abroad. The night is their time. Honest Englishmen will be indoors by nightfall. Remember that."

At Nottingham the next night we were treated like spies, simply because we were strangers. People in the streets stepped aside and watched us with narrowed eyes. When we finally reached our tavern we were questioned by the men in the taproom for news from the north. "Are the Scots on the Borders yet?" they demanded.

"Not yet," we assured them.

"They will be," they told us gloomily. "We're repairing the castle walls and putting up new platforms for the cannon."

A squint-eyed woman with dyed yellow hair said, "And you can tell that to your Scottish friends, if you're their spies. They won't take Nottingham without a fight."

"We're loyal English men," I told her.

"They all say that," she sneered. And it was true. Even Skeres and Frizer would have claimed that.

When we reached Stratford, Anne Shakespeare welcomed her husband with a kiss and a tight smile. If she was afraid for her daughter, she wasn't showing it. If she was blaming her husband's spying, she wasn't saying so.

She gave us the best meal we'd eaten since leaving Marsden Hall, and then said, "You've done well to find out where Judith is and to get back so quickly. But you're too tired now to think about helping our daughter. Have a good night's sleep and we'll decide what to do tomorrow."

None of us had the strength to argue. And Anne Shakespeare was right. She could see our exhaustion. I lay in a bed without fleas, under a roof without rats, for the first time in days. I slept like the dead and woke to find the sky had cleared. The sun slipped in and out of towering white clouds, but the air had a sharpness about it that told us summer was over and winter not too far away.

In the hall of New Place the sunlight fell in shafts that were broken by the lead that joined the small panes.

After breakfast Master Shakespeare stood with his back to the fire, the way Sir James did back at Marsden Hall. "Skeres wants me," he said simply. "Once he has me, Judith will be safe. It would be best if I rode out to the Hanged Man and gave myself up to him."

"Once he has you, he'll kill you *both*," I said.

"Well said, Meg," Anne nodded. "*You* may want to be a martyr, William Shakespeare, but a dead husband is as much use as a dead horse – you can't eat him and he won't earn you any money."

"Anyway," I went on, "it isn't only Anne that needs you. England needs you. We have to stop Skeres and keep you alive."

"And the English theatre needs you," Hugh Richmond said. "What on earth can Will Marsden and I do if we don't have your plays to perform?"

"So you can forget this idea of giving yourself up to Skeres in exchange for Judith," Anne said.

"Yes, my love," the playwright said humbly. "But perhaps I can be the bait in a trap to catch the man. If he comes after me, he'll have to leave Judith."

"That's true," I agreed. "Can we write him a message saying that you want to meet him somewhere? When he leaves the Hanged Man, we go in and set Judith free."

"Where do I meet him?" Master Shakespeare asked.

"You don't *have* to meet him," I told him. "You just *say* you want to meet him."

Anne shook her head slowly. "Even if you *do* set Judith free, it just leaves us where we were before you went to Marsden. William is in Stratford and Skeres will kill him at the first chance he gets. He will only be safe when he's protected by Cecil's men in London."

"So what do we do?" Hugh sighed.

"We get rid of Skeres," Anne Shakespeare said grimly.

"Kill him?" Will gasped. "We're not murderers."

"He's a dangerous man," she said. "As long as Elizabeth is alive, he'll be working to make sure England dies with her. Skeres has to die so that thousands can live. Don't you see that?"

"Anne!" Master Shakespeare wailed. "I'm an actor, not an assassin!"

"So am I!" Hugh added quickly.

"Look, Skeres will not rest until you are dead, William ... and you cannot rest until Skeres is dead," she said firmly.

Suddenly everything was clear to me. It struck me like a ray of the sun that beamed through the window of New Place and fell on some scripts on the table. "Then you have to die, Master Shakespeare," I said.

He looked at me curiously. Anne opened her mouth to object, but he held up a hand and said, "Yes, Meg. Go on."

"*Romeo and Juliet*," I said. "That play you told me about. The only way Juliet could escape was to take a drug and pretend she was dead. Perhaps that's the only way you'll be free of Skeres."

"But ..." Will began to object.

"Yes," Master Shakespeare said. "There is such a drug. They call it digitalis – it's made from the foxglove plant. It slows the heartbeat down so much that no doctor can feel it."

"There's a risk if you take too much of it," his wife said. "Your heart might slow to a stop."

"But there's a greater risk if I don't," he said. "*Romeo and Juliet!* I should have thought of it myself! Skeres must be told of my death, of course ..."

"I can do that," Hugh offered. "He's never seen me. He doesn't know I'm one of Sir Robert Cecil's most trusted spies."

"But ..." Will tried to interrupt.

"And I can set Judith free as soon as Skeres leaves her at the Hanged Man," I said. "I know exactly where the loft is."

"But ..." Will kept saying.

"Yes, Will, you can come with me."

"That's not what I'm trying to say!"

"So, say it now," I grinned.

"*Romeo and Juliet* is a *tragedy*! They both *die* in the end and no one ends up happy. I saw the play in Durham once. Their plan fails. There are bodies all over the stage!"

"Master Shakespeare is a playwright," I said. "He can write this story with a different ending if he wants to, can't you?"

He nodded. "I can."

"We'll plot it as carefully as you did with Frizer's trial. You'll see, this will be just as successful. We'll make sure nothing can go wrong."

Will sat at the table, buried his head in his hands and groaned. The trouble with him was that he had no faith in me, or my plans.

CHAPTER FIFTEEN

"To die, to sleep"

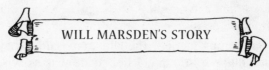

WILL MARSDEN'S STORY

Inside the cottage it was as dark as a cave. A black cat watched us as we entered the door, only its golden eyes showing in the weak light of a lantern.

The man looked up from the table where he was working, his eyes hidden behind the two glass disks of his spectacles. "Good morning," he said. His voice rustled like dry paper. "I believe you may want a love potion, young man. Am I right? I can see into the hearts of the people who walk through my door."

"We have a friend," Anne Shakespeare began. "A friend who is in danger of his life."

"And you want me to provide a cure? What is his sickness?" the man asked. "I can even cure the plague. Yes! It's the plague, isn't it? I can see it in your heart."

"He's in danger from an assassin's knife or crossbow bolt," I explained.

"Ah, then there is only one cure for that. Strike first and strike faster!" He hissed the "s" sounds and spittle from his lips sprayed into the thick air.

"We are not killers," Mistress Anne said. "We think the only way to escape the murderer is to imitate death before he arrives."

"A dangerous game," the old man said. They called him the village wise man. I hoped he was as wise as his name.

"There is a drug that calms the heart," I said.

He stretched his chicken neck forward. "I know!" he said. "I know."

"Do you have some?"

He lowered his head. "The punishment for selling poison is death," he whispered.

"We're not asking for poison!" I said.

"You *are*," he argued. "One drop will send a man to sleep. But two drops will kill him. If you're lying – if you use my drug to kill your friend – I will hang alongside you."

"You know we don't plan to use it as a poison," I said.

"Ah! But *how* do I know for sure?" he asked cleverly, his watery eyes blinking behind the blank disks of glass.

"Because you can see into our hearts," I reminded him.

"Oh! Yes. So I can ... but your hearts could be lying."

"So, you won't sell us the drug?" asked Anne Shakespeare.

"I didn't say that! I am simply telling you the risk I run," he hissed.

I understood. "You wish to be paid extra for the risk?"

"Why not?"

"How much?"

"Five pounds."

Anne Shakespeare gave a snorting laugh. "You want *five pounds* for the juice of a common flower that you found by the roadside?"

"No! I want five pounds for risking my neck in selling it to you."

She took a step forward and placed a hand on his table. "But your miserable neck isn't *worth* five pounds, Master Apothecary."

"It is to me!" he said.

"I will give you one pound."

"Four – and not one groat less," he told her, his thin hands clenched tight.

"Two pounds."

"Hah! Go and find your own foxgloves and distil them and feed your drug to your friend. Get the measure wrong and you'll kill him," the man sneered. His anger was rising. "But perhaps that doesn't matter! Since some assassin's going to kill him anyway, without my mixture! You may as well kill him yourself!"

"Three pounds," Anne Shakespeare said in a level voice.

"Three pounds? Three miserable pounds? You can't value your friend's life very highly if he's only worth three pounds. I want five or nothing!"

"You just said four," I pointed out.

"Did I? Very well, then. Four."

Anne stepped back from the table. "Will Marsden!"

"Yes, Mistress Shakespeare?"

"Take this creature's eyeglasses and crush them under the heel of your boot."

"Yes, Mistress Shakespeare."

I reached forward and he almost fell backwards off his

stool. "Three pounds!" he squawked.

"Three pounds it is," Mistress Shakespeare nodded. "And it's robbery even at that price."

The man took a stone jar from the shelf behind him. He measured some of the liquid into a small glass bottle, then carefully wiped up a spilled drop. He placed a stopper in the bottle and handed it to the woman. "One drop and your friend will sleep like the dead for a day. Two drops and he'll sleep like the dead ... forever. If he dies, I will deny that I sold you this drug."

"If he dies, you won't have to worry," Mistress Shakespeare said brightly. "My friend here will come back and kill you."

The man blinked wildly behind his glasses. "You said you weren't killers!"

"Ah, but this wouldn't be like killing a human. It would be like snuffing out the life of some miserable insect. It would be like crushing a beetle."

"The drug will work!" he said, but his voice was trembling now.

"It had better, Master Apothecary. It had better," she said, and threw three gold coins on his table.

The air outside was cold, but wonderfully fresh after the stuffy den we had just left. "What a strange man!" I said, as we mounted our horses to ride back to Stratford. "He's just like the apothecary in your husband's play, *Romeo and Juliet*."

Anne Shakespeare smiled. "Perhaps because he *is* the apothecary in my husband's play. Where do you think Master Shakespeare got the idea from?"

"From meeting that man? I see! And he's such a weird creature!"

"No, Will, he's a very *ordinary* little man. He went to school with my husband in the hall across the road from New Place."

"But all that magic! The power to see into our hearts."

"Hah! He can no more see into your heart than you can see into the moon. That little man is just another actor, like Hugh Richmond and my husband. No one would buy love potions and corn cures from a man who looks like the local priest. They want to believe he's a magician, so he has to act like one." She stopped her horse and looked at me. "Don't believe everything you see, Will Marsden. And don't believe everything people tell you."

"No, Mistress Shakespeare."

We rode on in silence for a while and then I said, "But if he's a fraud and an actor, his sleeping drug won't work."

"Some of his potions and mixtures have been handed down for hundreds of years – and this is one of them. It has lasted down the ages because it *does* work. I'm not sure about the love potions or the plague cures he sells. But Master Shakespeare and I have seen this drug work. Where do you think my husband got the idea for his play?"

I nodded. "So it's safe."

"Oh, it's far from safe, Will. We are risking my husband's life. But life is full of risks."

The village where the apothecary had his shop was five miles outside Stratford. It was dinner time before we arrived back at New Place. Meg and Hugh had already set off to the Hanged Man to try to rescue Judith.

Master Shakespeare had been working hard while we were away. He was dressed in a white shroud and his neck was painted with purple plague marks. "Juice from blackcurrants," he said. His eyes were rimmed with red and his skin deathly white between the plague spots.

The town carpenter was just finishing the lid of his coffin. "We have the liquid," Anne said quietly.

"I will take it now," the playwright said. "When I fall asleep you must announce my death in the town. If Skeres comes to see my corpse, it would be good if my death is being talked about."

"Yes, husband."

"And I have sent the steward to have the family vault opened at Holy Trinity Church. I need to be placed in the vault tonight." He turned to me. "Will, I have written this epitaph for myself. Take it to a stonemason and have my tombstone carved with these words."

"But you are not going to die!" I exclaimed.

His eyes widened. "We are all going to die, Will ... some time. I would like this to be ready for that day. I may live through this, and I may survive Skeres's dagger, but I'll need it one day."

I picked up the parchment where he had written a verse in his sloping, looping writing:

Good friend, for Jesus' sake forbear
To dig the dust enclosed here.
Blessed be the man that spares these stones,
And cursed be he that moves my bones.

It was a curious thing to write. I felt overcome with the sadness of his death before it had happened. Then I was shaken by the fear his death might be closer than we knew. Anne, too, was looking bleak and miserable.

The playwright smiled at us. "It's all just a dream,

Anne," he said. "We are all made of dreams and our life ends with a little sleep."

"What will I do if you die?" she asked.

"What would I do if *you* died?" he asked. "Or Judith?" He looked like a ghost in his dreadful make-up and corpse sheet.

"I'm not sure if I'm awake or if I'm dreaming this," said his wife.

"We're used to doing both at the same time when we're on stage, aren't we, Will? Living a dream – that's what acting is," Master Shakespeare said.

"Yes, Master Shakespeare," I answered.

Suddenly he said, "I wonder if Kit Marlowe did this?"

"Pretended he was dead?" I asked.

"Yes. He was in danger of his life. Yet at the vital moment he died."

"He was stabbed in the eye."

"Was he? How do we know that for sure?"

"The magistrates would have examined the body and seen the wound. You can't fake a stab in the eye," I argued.

"We faked heads being cut off and hands being lopped," he reminded me.

"I know, but ... but that was in the theatre. We used shadows and fast movements like some conjuror at a fair."

He looked disappointed. "I always hoped that Marlowe was living on somewhere. Perhaps you're right, Will. But at least one part of Marlowe will live forever. His plays will live on."

"And so will yours," I told him. "So will yours."

"You think so?"

"I do."

The thought cheered him and he turned to his wife. "So, now the drug."

She took the bottle from her purse and carefully placed one drop in a hollow in the glass stopper. Master Shakespeare raised it to the light as if he were examining a fine wine. "*'Here's drink. I drink to thee!'*" he said. "That's what Juliet said before she drank the drug."

He sipped the drop from the glass and tasted it on his tongue. He shivered a little. Then he walked over to his coffin, climbed into it and lay back. He arranged the shroud neatly round his neck, then folded his arms across his chest.

His large brown eyes were bright in the afternoon sunlight that flowed into the room. "*'Farewell. God knows when we shall meet again,'*" he murmured, repeating more of Juliet's farewell speech. Then his eyelids began to droop. His next words were mumbled like a man who talks in his sleep. "*'I have a faint cold fear thrills through my veins ... that almost freezes up the heat of life.'*"

Then the eyes closed. Under the ghastly make-up his skin turned a more natural and deadly shade of white. His chest stopped moving and his mouth fell open.

Anne Shakespeare stared at the figure in the coffin for a long time. Finally she crossed to the door and called for the steward who had returned from the church. "Go to the mayor's house and tell him Master William Shakespeare is dead. Tell him the burial will be this evening at Holy Trinity. We need a swift burial – and no visitors – because Master Shakespeare had the plague. He brought it from London. We will bury my husband tonight, then we will shut ourselves in New Place for a week to be sure we don't spread the disease."

The steward gave a bow and went to follow Mistress Shakespeare's orders. She looked at me. "And now, we wait."

I passed the bright afternoon reading some of the manuscripts the playwright had collected in a great chest. I didn't know how one head could hold so many stories, so much poetry, so many characters and so many words.

The doctor arrived at dusk, a fat man with a healthy pink face and white hair. He looked into the coffin, but refused to touch the body. The man knew nothing of our plan – we decided it would be better that way. But fear of the plague kept him from examining Master Shakespeare too closely. He held a mirror to the mouth of our corpse and then looked at it. There was no mist on the mirror. He shook his head. "I am sorry, Mistress Shakespeare … perhaps if you had called me earlier."

"My husband knew he was beyond help," she said. "He did not want to trouble you."

The man nodded nervously, his chins wobbling. He backed towards the door. "My sympathy to you and your daughters," he said. He almost stumbled into the street in his hurry to leave.

"The doctor said he was dead," Anne Shakespeare said quietly.

"The doctor said that because he was too frightened to do his job," I said. "It's the way we planned it. Everything is going to plan."

"What if he wakes up too soon? What if he finds himself in the crypt with all his dead relatives? It's enough to frighten any man to death!"

"When the coffin's been placed in the crypt, I'll go back and watch, shall I? Just in case."

"Would you, Will?"

"Of course. It's a sensible thing to do."

"It's something I should do," she said.

"No. Someone may be watching the house. We don't know. If you leave and go to sit in a stone chamber they will suspect something. But no one will follow me. I'll wait till the darkest hour and slip out of the house by the orchard gate."

She looked at me, her eyes creased with the effort of holding back tears. "I had a son," she said. "He's in the crypt where they'll be putting my husband's coffin."

"I know."

"My Hamnet. He was about your age now, Will. I wish he could have had the opportunity to be as brave as you. Your father must be proud of you."

I didn't feel brave. I wanted to be home in my room in Marsden Hall. Instead I was going to spend the night in a room full of bones with a man who was scarcely breathing. But I was an actor. I had to act brave to keep Mistress Shakespeare's spirits high.

I had no idea what Meg and Hugh were doing, or how successful they had been. The plan seemed simple enough, yet I was sure something would go wrong.

Four coffin-bearers arrived, wearing black cloaks and masks over the bottom halves of their faces. They lifted the open coffin on to a wagon draped in black and pulled by two black horses. Two of the men walked ahead of the horses, carrying torches whose flames whipped and flickered in the cold night air. We walked behind down Chapel Lane.

The bell on Holy Trinity Church began to ring its slow, sad note. The priest came out as we reached the gate into the churchyard and said some hurried prayers. No mourners had turned out to see this funeral. Plague victims went to their graves without a farewell from their living friends.

The coffin was taken down stone steps into the underground chamber and the lid put in place. Anne Shakespeare gave a little cry.

"The carpenter has made sure the coffin is not sealed," I

said. "And I'll be back in a few hours to take the lid off again."

Mistress Shakespeare nodded and leaned on my arm as I led her away from the gruesome place. We returned to New Place and paid the coffin-bearers and the wagon driver for their services. By the time they had left and the steward had given us hot wine, Anne Shakespeare had recovered some of her spirits. Drinking the wine warmed me, but it also made me drowsy. I nodded by the fire and had a nightmare of graves opening and skeletons rising. One of them stretched out a hand towards me and gripped my arm. I cried out and a voice said, "Will! It's one o'clock!"

I peered up into Mistress Shakespeare's pale face. "Thanks," I said. "I'll get to the graveyard now."

I took one of the thickest cloaks she could find. It was long enough for me to wrap all round my legs if I had to sit in that cold crypt the rest of the long, dark morning. "Take this sword," she said, offering me a fine steel blade. "Now that he's a gentleman, he can wear this sword. He's proud of that."

I buckled the sword round my waist, where it hung clumsily. Anne Shakespeare gave me a lantern with a fresh wax candle and I set off through the orchard where the trees creaked in the wind and the dying leaves rattled over my head.

I picked my way carefully over the gutters that were trickling down the middle of the street. The water was fresh enough after the recent showers, but I didn't want to be sitting on guard with soaking feet.

The streets were empty apart from roaming dogs rooting in rubbish heaps, and they ran off into the shadows when they saw me coming. Clouds covered the half-moon. In small breaks between the clouds, darker shadows blotted out the stars as bats flew down from the church tower on some secret, silent hunt.

The church gate creaked slightly as I pushed it open. I held up my lantern to find my path and the gate swung to suddenly in the wind and struck it. My hands were cold and they stung when the gate hit the lantern. That's why I dropped it.

The candle went out and left me in almost total darkness. I didn't know how I'd find the crypt without a light, let alone Master Shakespeare's coffin. Suppose I found one in the dark and opened it by mistake? What horror would I find in there?

The thought frightened me, so, just for a moment, I was pleased to see that light from a candle spilled out of the open door to the crypt. Just for a moment. Then I realized that the candlelight meant just one thing.

Someone was there before me. That someone could be making quite sure that Master Shakespeare was dead! What could I do? I reached for the sword that hung at my belt. My hand fell on the hilt and gripped it.

Then another hand came from behind me. It was clammy with sweat and it clasped my sword hand tight ...

CHAPTER SIXTEEN

"The glimpses of the moon making night hideous"

HUGH RICHMOND'S STORY

I am an actor, you understand. I am not a fine writer like Will Marsden, or a born storyteller like Meg Lumley. I am an *actor*. But Will and Meg insist that I'm the only one who can tell this part of the story.

Oh, well, here goes.

The plan was that Meg and I would ride south out of Stratford and then turn east, and I would approach the Hanged Man from the Banbury road as if I'd just ridden from that town. Meg would wait in a copse of trees until I signalled with a wave of my yellow silk handkerchief. While I kept Nicholas Skeres busy, she would slip round to the stables and set free Judith Shakespeare. A simple plan.

I am *not* blaming Meg for the fact that we got a little lost. But it might have been quicker to get to the Hanged Man by way of Dundee rather than the way we went.

"It's this map," she complained. Mistress Shakespeare had drawn it for us before we left.

"Perhaps it's upside down," I suggested.

She glared at me with those fierce green eyes – then

turned it the right way up. I said nothing. The truth is I hardly dared say a word to cross her. Meg was in a determined mood.

It was growing dark by the time we reached the small wood where Meg would hide. "Will you see my handkerchief in this light?" I asked.

"Hugh," she said rudely, "you could see that buttercup-coloured nose-wipe if you buried it a mile underground."

"It's fashionable," I told her.

"It's ridiculous," she said.

Meg could be very hurtful, although, of course, she never hurt me! I made sure she was armed with a sharp knife in case Judith needed to be cut free. Then she left her horse hidden in the trees and watched me ride down the road.

There was a man standing on the front doorstep of the tavern. He wore a patch over his right eye. His left eye watched me the way a blackbird watches a worm.

The tavern itself was so shabby that I would never have stayed there by choice. The painted picture of the hanged man swung in the cold breeze and creaked as if the gallows themselves held a corpse. I shuddered – with *disgust*, not fear, you understand.

"Good evening, sir!" I cried cheerfully. I did not feel cheerful, but I acted the part and I am a fine actor ... as I think I may have mentioned.

He grunted in reply.

I went on, "I was heading for Stratford, but I became a little lost after I left Banbury. I won't make it before nightfall. Do you have a room in your fine tavern to let?"

"It's not my tavern," he said. "It

belongs to a man called Frizer. I'm looking after it while he's in the north."

"But you can let me have a bed?"

"I suppose so."

"And a little food?"

"If you don't mind sharing my rabbit pie," he shrugged.

As the man turned his back on me, I pulled out my beautiful silk handkerchief and waved it in the direction of the wood.

Skeres led the way into the cramped and dingy taproom where a few gloomy villagers were hunched over the cloudy ale. I said I'd have some wine with my pie. He served me some thin stuff that was more water than vinegar and more vinegar than wine.

I talked about London and about Queen Elizabeth's health. I even tried to get Skeres talking about the Hanged Man and his partner, but he showed little interest.

I must have kept up my one-sided conversation for an hour, but he just looked bored. I can't imagine *why*. I am the most charming of talkers and my London friends love me for my wit and cleverness. The villagers were looking at me wide-eyed. They had never seen anyone so well spoken as I was. They had never seen anyone so well *dressed* either. I was wearing my best brown velvet doublet with a yellow silk lining made of the same material as my handkerchief. Even after several hours in the saddle I must have been a fine and handsome sight.

Will and I had agreed that I would keep Skeres talking as long as possible so that Meg would have time to free Judith. When he began to yawn and move towards the back door, I went into the speech that Will and I had rehearsed.

"Terrible news from Stratford about Master William Shakespeare," I said.

Skeres paused with his hand on the latch and turned. His eye burned into me. "What's that, friend?"

"Haven't you heard? The greatest loss to the English theatre since Thomas Kyd died!"

"What are you talking about, man?" Skeres growled.

I dabbed at my lips with my handkerchief and told him. "I was in Banbury, on my way to join Master William Shakespeare. He's a sharer in the Globe Theatre in London, where I perform. I am one of his leading actors, you know. The Queen herself said she was overcome with grief when I died on stage."

"What about Shakespeare?" Skeres said rudely.

"Of course, I didn't *really* die on stage. I was playing the part of Hamlet – the hero of one of the greatest plays by this country's greatest playwright."

"Some say," the man sneered. "But what has happened to him?"

"Oh? Didn't I tell you? I was sitting in the dining room of Banbury's finest tavern eating roasted capon in the most delicious tarragon sauce. I'll swear the cream came from the cows of heaven!"

"Get on with the story, man!" Skeres said. The scar on his cheek was turning purple with anger.

"But this *is* my story, good sir! A merchant from Stratford arrived and sat at my table – he could see I was the sort of elegant person he would want to share a meal with. I told him I was going to meet Master Shakespeare in Stratford and his words sent a chill to my heart like a blade of cold, Spanish steel. I shall remember them until my dying day."

"Your dying day may be sooner than you think, if you don't tell me what he said," Skeres snarled.

"He said, 'You won't be meeting William Shakespeare anywhere, this side of heaven!' I gasped when I understood what he meant! 'Is the great man dead?' I asked. 'As dead as that chicken you've just eaten,' he told me."

Skeres's bright eye lit up. "He's been murdered at last," he murmured.

"Murdered? Good lord, sir, no! He had a fever – the merchant thinks it may have been the sweating sickness – and he died earlier today. The townsfolk are so afraid of the plague they wanted him buried at once. They say he brought it with him from the London theatres. Master Shakespeare was going to rest in his family crypt at Holy Trinity Church this evening."

"Dead? Shakespeare is dead?" Skeres breathed. "I don't believe it."

"But you *must*, my dear sir," I told him. "I will leave here at dawn tomorrow and visit the grave before the crypt is sealed up again. I must pay my respects to that brilliant man."

"Not so *very* brilliant," Skeres jeered. "He couldn't save himself or his family."

"His family?" I asked.

Skeres lowered his head to hide his confusion. "I've heard his daughter has been kidnapped," he muttered.

"Ah, then the kidnappers can let her go now, I suppose. Dead men pay no ransoms!"

"Once they are *sure* that the father is dead ... I suppose," he admitted.

"But he *is* dead!" I cried.

"Have you seen the corpse?" Skeres growled.

"No ... but ..."

"Neither have I. And I won't believe it until I do."

"Then come with me tomorrow morning, my friend. I'll enjoy your cheerful company at this time of great sadness," I said.

"No!" said Skeres and made for the front door. "I'll go *now*."

"They won't let you over Clopton Bridge into the town at this time of night!"

"There are ways," was all he said.

He slammed the door behind him, but it jammed. It took me a minute or two, with the help of the villagers, to tear it open. I ran into the road to see him vanishing into the darkness ... and he had taken my horse.

I leapt back into the tavern, collected a lantern and lit it from one of the filthy tallow candles on the wall. Then I hurried across the back courtyard to where I guessed the stables must be. There were only the two bony old nags that Meg and Will had brought from London.

I looked up at the loft. Meg and Judith should have been gone an hour ago. The trapdoor to the loft was closed, but not bolted. I guessed they'd gone. "Judith?" I called softly. "Judith Shakespeare?"

There was a scuffle that was probably a rat and then silence. I looked around the stable, but could see no

saddles or bridles for the horses. The creatures were too bony to ride bareback. And, anyway, I didn't think they could raise a trot. I could see why Skeres had taken my horse.

I decided to run back to Stratford. It was only five miles, the roads were soft, but not deep in mud, and I was strong. Most people forget that an actor spends hours on stage every day using his lungs and needs to be tireless. My Hamlet went on for four hours! A five-mile trot would be easy for me.

I left the quiet stable yard behind me and began to run steadily down the road to Stratford. No one from the village followed and I knew that only Skeres would be ahead of me. He couldn't gallop on an unlit road, or the horse could stumble and break its leg. A stumble could also break Skeres's neck.

Skeres would beat me back to Stratford, but not by a great deal.

The night birds screeched over my head when they heard my padding feet. Sheep bleated in the roadside fields and ran away from me, but no humans tried to stop me. At each crossroads I stopped to catch my breath. I used a flint to light the signposts and guide me on my way.

I reached one final signpost and stopped. I don't know if I heard the ghost first, or if I remembered the stories first and *then* heard the ghost. But there was a rattle of chains. I knew that crossroads were the haunts of poor lost souls in torment. People who killed themselves were buried at crossroads. An old wise woman once explained it to me, "The crossroads post is driven through the heart so the ghost is trapped in its grave. But, if the spirit does rise up, it will be confused by the ends of four roads and not know which way to turn."

I didn't believe that nonsense, you understand. But I challenge you to stand at a crossroads in the deepest, darkest hours of night and not feel a little uneasy. The sound of a trotting horse and the rattle of chains were enough to warn me to be careful. I dived into the nearest hedgerow. This was a foolish thing to do, I thought, as the brambles tore at my expensive doublet and ripped velvet and silk beyond repair.

I turned in time to see two ghastly figures ride by. A little man – probably a goblin, I thought – holding the reins and a poor young woman rattling her chains and hanging on behind. The woman's hair was wild as dandelion seed and her face stained and smirched by the fires of Hell.

They were gone along the Stratford road as quickly as they had appeared.

It took me a few minutes to drag myself out of the hedge and, I don't mind telling you, I was a little shaken. Walking on I found I was just a few minutes from Clopton Bridge at the edge of Stratford.

I guessed that the whole journey had taken me just over an hour. After the fright of the devil riders from Hell, I was disturbed to see something moving in the darkness ahead of me.

The moon slipped out from behind a cloud and I saw it clearly. It was my own horse, abandoned and grazing quietly by the roadside. Skeres had decided that it would be easier to slip into town without it. He could be right. The night watch would be half asleep, as usual, and would miss any man who let himself be hidden by the moon shadows. But even the Stratford watch couldn't miss a man on a horse.

I crouched below the parapet of Clopton Bridge as I hurried across, then turned sharp left at the end. I avoided the streets by walking along the riverside path and came to the churchyard wall around Holy Trinity about ten minutes after entering the town.

Someone was standing at the gate of the churchyard. A slim young man with a sword so long it almost trailed along the ground. He held a lantern and pushed open the gate.

I pulled my dagger from my belt and turned it so the point was towards my face. I could strike the young man over the back of the head if he looked like harming the sleeping playwright.

I hurried silently over the soft grass until I was close enough to touch him. The gate was caught by the wind and swung to, striking his lantern hand. The lantern fell and the candle went out.

He gasped. He looked up and we both saw the light in the crypt at the same time. But, in the moment before the lantern was dashed to the ground, I had seen enough of his face to know that I was standing behind Will Marsden. He reached for the hilt of his sword and stepped towards the light. The gallant young idiot had decided to tackle the murderous Skeres alone!

I reached out and grasped the hand he'd placed on the

sword. As I did so I felt the cold, sharp prick of a knife-point pressing against the back of my neck. "Lay one finger on him and I'll cut your head off," the voice said ...

CHAPTER SEVENTEEN

"Freeze thy young blood"

MEG LUMLEY'S STORY

I had a bad feeling from the start about the rescue of Judith Shakespeare. Getting a little lost didn't matter too much. It meant that we were going to be working under the cover of darkness. But I shivered in the wood as I watched Hugh Richmond ride down the hill towards the Hanged Man Tavern.

The plan depended on our working together. Will had to make sure the funeral went smoothly, then watch the crypt in case Master Shakespeare woke early, or his enemies arrived too soon.

Hugh had to keep Nicholas Skeres busy while I released Judith and took her back to her mother's safekeeping. Then Hugh had to stay with Skeres as he went to check on the body the next morning.

Hugh waved his absurd yellow handkerchief and I ran down into the village. I slipped straight to the stables at the back of the Hanged Man where our old horses stood dozing. One of them gave a soft whinny as I stroked its muzzle. A lantern hung from a hook and gave a faint light. I took it down and looked around the stable. At the far end a ladder led up to a trapdoor in the hay loft.

I climbed carefully, each rung creaking, till I reached

the top. There was a new iron bolt on the outside of the trapdoor. That would only make sense if someone *outside* the loft wanted to keep someone *in*. And I didn't think Skeres was afraid of his hay supply running away.

The bolt was stiff and I couldn't move it. I climbed back down the ladder and found a hay fork propped against the wall. It would make a good weapon, I decided. The wooden handle made a useful hammer as I tapped at the bolt and slowly loosened it. At last the bolt slid free and I pushed the trapdoor up.

There were angry squeals as I disturbed the rats that had been lying on top of the trapdoor. I pushed again and stepped up till my head and shoulders were through the opening. When I lifted the lantern I found the frightened face of a girl staring back at me. Her large brown eyes were terrified. She was a little older than me. Her hair was tangled and full of hay stalks and her face had not been washed for days. Still, there was no doubt that this was Master Shakespeare's daughter.

I placed a finger to my lips and climbed into the loft beside her. I lowered the trapdoor back into place and sat next to her. "Judith?"

She nodded. "Who are you?"

"My name's Meg. Meg Lumley. I'm a friend of your father's. I've come to take you home."

Her eyes had heavy lids, like Master Shakespeare's, and now they filled with tears. "I thought you were Skeres coming to kill me," she whispered.

"No. An actor called Hugh Richmond is keeping Skeres busy while you and I ride back to Stratford."

"I can't!" she said.

"I'll help you."

"But I'm fastened here. Look, there's a chain around my waist and it's fixed into the wall with a staple. Can you snap the chain?"

I groaned. I knew that there would be problems we hadn't foreseen. I had guessed Judith might be *tied*, but not *chained*. There was a lock on the chain, but only Skeres would have the key. Judith reached out both hands and clutched at my arms. "But thank you for trying. At least I won't die alone."

"You won't die at all!" I said fiercely. I began to explain the plan we had to save her and her father. She trembled at the thought of Master Shakespeare taking the drug.

"And you think he'll return and set me free once he believes my father's dead?" she asked.

"We're not sure. He may not want any witnesses to this kidnapping. He may return and kill you. That's why we wanted to free you first."

"But you can't," she sighed.

"I'll find a way," I said.

I traced the chain back to the wall. The heavy staple was deep inside the wood. But, like an aching tooth, it could be torn free from its roots if it was jiggled from side to side. "Can you pull on the chain?" I asked Judith.

"I've been trying for days," she said. "But I'm weak. He's been feeding me bread and water."

"And when you need the jakes?" I asked.

"He's left a bucket in the corner," she told me. "I can just reach it." She gripped my arm again. "That's not the worst. The worst are the rats. They smell the bread and they come to steal it. Everyday they are getting bolder.

Tonight they tried to take it from my hand as I put it to my mouth. And when I fall asleep I wake to find them sniffing at my throat. I think they're just waiting for me to die. I'm going to be their next meal!"

I held her hands for a while and told her I understood her fears, but her troubles were over now. "If we both pull the chain together," I suggested. She gave a weak smile and sat up. We wrapped our hands around the thick iron links and heaved. I strained till I could feel the blood pounding in my head and hear Judith gasping with the effort. After a minute I stopped. Sweat was making my hands slip off the chain and my palms were being scraped raw on the rough metal.

I checked the staple. It hadn't moved. Judith was looking tired, yet her spirits were rising. "If you could put something into the loop of the staple, maybe you could lever it out."

I remembered the hay fork. Perfect. The final point of the fork fitted into the metal loop and the long handle meant I had a good grip. I jammed the point into the staple and began to swing on the handle. It was springy and I could have sworn that I felt some movement. The problem was that I wasn't heavy enough. I jumped in the air,

tucked up my legs and swung on the handle with every ounce of my weight.

That was the moment the shaft chose to splinter and snap. I fell on the hay, stumbled backwards on to the trap-door and felt it bend and crack under the impact of my fall, but I didn't break through. I lay there panting for several minutes and thanked my lucky stars that I'd closed that trapdoor. I was aching with painful bruises to my hip and shoulder, but it could have been worse – I could have been lying ten feet down with a broken neck.

I finally sat up. Judith's eyes showed that she shared the pain of the failure. I wished someone could have shared the pain of the fall. "Thanks, Meg, you tried."

There are some people who fail and give up. For some reason I've never been like that. When I fail I get angry and more determined than ever. I rubbed my hip to find out why it hurt so much. It was the handle of my knife which I'd landed on. I pulled it out to rub the soreness beneath the belt and stopped. "Of course!" I said. "It's simple!"

Judith nodded. "Of course," she said. "We can take it in turns."

And we started to cut at the wooden wall that held the staple. The knife was good and the wood was old, but still it took an hour of patient paring and chipping to dig down to the root of the staple. Sweat ran into my eyes and made the boy's hose I was wearing stick to me. My bruised shoulder ached and my hands were scratched and bleeding. But my reward was seeing Judith's strength grow with her hopes.

After an hour the staple was moving in its socket like a loose tooth. I looked at her. "Now we try pulling again?"

She nodded eagerly. I wrapped my doublet round the chain to get a better grip and spare my hands. We pulled together and I felt Judith's effort twice as strong as before. In a minute the staple sprang from the wall and we lay back exhausted on the straw. Then, over the sound of our breathing, we heard the horses shuffling in their stalls below us and footsteps on the cobbles. For Skeres to catch us now was just too cruel.

"Judith?" the voice called up. "Judith Shakespeare?"

Her throat was as frozen in terror as mine was. I wondered if I could push the staple back into the wall, hide beneath a pile of straw and blow out the candle. He would check on Judith and maybe go away. But I knew it was hopeless. Once he found the bolt undone, he would come up and check the whole lot. When he saw the staple cut out, he'd know there was someone there and he'd find me. It was so unfair I wanted to scream.

Then we heard the footsteps again, but this time they were hurrying away across the stable yard. I'll swear my heart had stopped as still as Master Shakespeare's in his coffin. Judith was free and the man had gone.

Of course she was still attached to a length of chain that was wrapped round her waist and fell to the floor. We'd have to carry that with us. She tried to stand. "My legs are weak," she said. She would have had trouble moving even without the chain. It was going to be a difficult journey back to Stratford. I took the weight of the

chain and opened the trapdoor. I backed on to the steps
and helped her shaking legs find their way down. It took
a long time for us to reach the floor.

"These horses are too slow," I said. "And someone
might hear us taking them out. I've got a good horse in
the wood just outside the village. I can't fetch it because
Skeres might hear it and come out. You'll have to walk a
quarter mile to where I've left it."

"I can do that," she said brightly.

We set off through the stable yard. No matter how we
tried the chain clanked and rattled. The inn was quiet. No
one came out to see what the noise was.

The journey to the wood was hard for Judith, but she
didn't complain. She may have had her father's looks, but
she had her mother's strength.

I tightened the girth on my horse's saddle and helped
Judith and her chain into it. Then I climbed in front of her
and took the bridle. The horse trotted briskly down the
hill. We slowed to a careful walk as we passed through the
sleeping village so the chain wouldn't rattle. Then we
moved quickly down the road to Stratford.

We met no one, though I thought I saw a figure in the
clouded moonlight as we came to a crossroads. The figure

seemed to hear our approach and vanished into a hedgerow. Ghosts haunt crossroads, I know. I was sure that must be a ghost, yet there was a snapping of twigs as the poor soul crashed through the hedge. I didn't think ghosts could disturb something as solid as a bush.

I said nothing to Judith, but rode on to Stratford. A horse grazed quietly at the end of Clopton Bridge. It looked very much like Hugh Richmond's horse, though I was sure he would stay at the Hanged Man with Skeres. It worried me. I was an hour or so late in freeing Judith. Perhaps Hugh's part of the plan had gone wrong too.

I slid down from the horse and led it over the bridge into Stratford. A watchman called out, "Who's there?" His voice was trembling with fear.

"Just two harmless ghosts, watchman. We're running away from Hell. Can you tell us the way to Heaven?" I asked.

Judith rattled her chains and gave a long low moan. The watchman didn't reply. We heard the clatter of his footsteps and a strange whimper.

I turned left into High Street and on into Chapel Street. A lantern glowed at the door of New Place and it was flung open as soon as I rapped. The steward helped Judith down from the horse, then led it away to a stable while I helped her into the main hall of the house.

Anne Shakespeare walked across the room and wrapped her arms around her daughter. She seemed unable to find any words. She looked up and stretched out one arm to wrap it around me too. Her grip on my bruised shoulder was painful, but I didn't complain. The pain had been worth it. I had completed my part of the plan and the joy of the mother and daughter were my reward.

"Where's Will?" I asked.

"At the crypt," Anne said. "He left by the orchard gate just before you arrived at the front door."

"I'll go and see if he is all right," I said.

"No! You have played your part, Meg. Let Will play his."

I didn't want to worry her. I didn't tell her about the mystery of Hugh Richmond's horse at Clopton Bridge. But I knew I'd never sleep while Will was alone with a sleeping playwright and a dozen corpses for company.

I left New Place by the orchard. There was a big enough moon for me to see my way down Chapel Lane. I picked my way carefully past the muck heaps that spilled into the roadway. I didn't need moonlight to see them when I could smell the rotting waste.

The church stood black and solid against the deep-purple sky. I saw Will ahead of me with his lantern, walking towards the gate of the churchyard. I was about to call softly to him when I saw a shadow move from the corner of the churchyard wall. Someone had come up from the riverside path and was hurrying up behind Will. If I called out to warn him, the man might decide to kill my friend on the spot before turning his sword on me.

Skeres, if that's who it was, didn't know I was behind him. His eyes must have been fixed on Will's back. If the shadowed stranger moved to draw his sword, *then* I would cry out, I decided, and I hurried to get as close to him as I could.

What came next happened very quickly. Will swung open the gate and looked into the churchyard. The wind swung the gate shut and knocked the lantern from his hand. I was ten yards from the gate. The man moved smoothly behind Will and looked over his shoulder. At that moment they both paused and looked towards the church. I saw the light an instant after they did and I drew my dagger. The stranger had drawn his own dagger and was ready to use it as a club.

Will reached for his sword, and the stranger shot out a hand to stop him from drawing it. I leapt forward and placed my dagger at the man's neck. "Lay one finger on him and I'll cut your head off," I said.

At that instant a breeze blew and drifted a faint, sweet scent into my nostrils, and then I knew who the strange man was ...

CHAPTER EIGHTEEN

"Yet now I must confess"

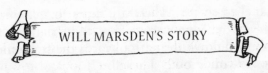

WILL MARSDEN'S STORY

When I reached for my sword and felt that damp hand over mine, I felt sure I'd be joining Master Shakespeare's relatives in the cold vault. Then, a moment later, I heard Meg's voice say, "Lay one finger on him and I'll cut your head off."

The man relaxed his grip on my hand and said, "I mean him no harm!" It was Hugh Richmond's voice. It took us a little while to sort out the confusion. We had reached the gate almost together. Hugh had been trying to stop me rushing into the crypt and Meg had been trying to stop Hugh from murdering me.

"So who's in the crypt?" I asked.

"Skeres," Hugh explained and quickly told his story of the spy stealing his horse and getting to Stratford first.

"It took me a long time to get Judith free," Meg said. "I must have passed you on the road, Hugh."

"Ah! Yes, I saw you!" he said and his teeth showed faintly in a grin. "I thought you might be friends of Skeres's. You're lucky I didn't challenge you and drag you out of the saddle."

Meg glared at him. "Difficult, Hugh, when your head was buried in the hedge."

"I *was* hiding there, but I was looking out!" he said.

"Then you must have eyes in your backside, because that's all I could see," she spat back. "Now, what are we going to do?"

"It's three to one," I said. "We can't let Skeres stay there much longer. If Master Shakespeare as much as stirs in his sleep then Skeres will kill him."

"Then let's go," Meg said.

"What's the plan?"

She laughed softly. "There are times for planning and times for action. Whatever we do will be right," she said as she stepped down the path towards the stone tomb.

"How do you know?" I asked.

She pulled a stone out of her purse and held it up to the light that glowed in the crypt. The stone had a hole worn through the centre. I knew it was what is called an elf-cup.

"Sometimes you have to trust to luck," said Meg.

"If Skeres is going to kill us all, then he'll *do* it," I agreed. "If it *isn't* meant to be, then he won't. Either way it won't help to waste hours worrying about it. It's like Master Shakespeare says, we are all just dreams and our little life ends with sleep."

Meg stopped me by resting a hand on my arm. "I'm so tired, Will. I feel like I've been on a journey to the edge of the world. And now I'm just one last step away from it."

"I know how you feel," I said. "Let's leap over the edge and see what happens."

"You're right," Hugh sighed. "Get it over with. One way or another."

He stood on the other side of Meg and linked his arm through hers. She didn't move until she'd said one more thing. "If I am going to die in there, I can't think of anyone I'd rather die with than my two friends."

She moved forward. Hugh and I held on to an arm each, and let her lead us into the house of death.

Skeres was sitting on a stone coffin and looking down at Master Shakespeare, whose coffin lay on the floor, the lid removed. Skeres was dressed in black, his face was as grey as the stone walls around him and only the lantern's yellow glow gave any colour to the scene in front of us. He looked up without surprise and said, "Good evening ... or I should say, good morning?"

"What are you doing here, sir?" Hugh asked in his powerful "Titus" voice. "Have you no respect for the dead?"

Skeres gave a twisted smile. "Oh, yes!" he said, glancing into the playwright's coffin. "And for the living."

"Master Shakespeare is sleeping with his dead ancestors," Hugh said sternly.

Skeres threw back his head and laughed suddenly. "Hah! The difference is the dead ancestors will not wake up."

"Nor will Master Shakespeare," Hugh said.

Skeres rose slowly, like a black cat stretching. "Really? Why is that?"

"Because he is dead," I said. My throat was tight.

"Then you won't mind if I push this dagger into his heart," Skeres said. A dagger glinted in his hand and his movement had been so quick I hadn't even seen him draw it.

"That's murder!" Meg cried.

Skeres opened his one good eye in wonder. "I don't think so. This man is here because a doctor has said that he is dead. How can I murder a dead man?"

None of us had an answer. Skeres went on. "I did think it strange that he is wearing make-up!" he said, wiping a finger over the purple colouring on the playwright's neck. "You know, of course, that a corpse doesn't bleed if it's cut after death? Shall we see what happens if we make a little cut on your friend's thumb?"

He lifted Master Shakespeare's hand and pushed the point of his dagger into the thumb. Blood streamed from the cut. Skeres rubbed the sticky liquid between his own thumb and finger. "Now, why do you think that would happen? Shall I tell you? It happened because Master Shakespeare is in a drugged sleep. He is not dead – and I am not so easily fooled. It's an old trick that our friend the corpse used in his *Romeo and Juliet* play."

"You've seen the play?" I asked. Somehow I couldn't believe that a spy would know the plays of Shakespeare.

Skeres gave a thin smile. "I've seen the play. And it ends in tragedy – just as this one will end in tragedy."

"If you kill Master Shakespeare, we will kill you in revenge – just like in Master Shakespeare's *Titus Andronicus*," Hugh threatened.

Skeres snorted. "And my friend Ingram Frizer will kill you in revenge for *my* death, and so it will go on till there is no one left alive!"

"No," Meg said. "We have already dealt with your friend Frizer."

The spy's hand tightened on his dagger. "No. He

wouldn't be beaten by a boy, a girl and a bag-of-wind actor!"

"You kidnapped Judith Shakespeare and bullied Anne Shakespeare into telling you where we were going. While you guarded Judith, Frizer went north to deal with us. But we're back here now, aren't we? Frizer must have failed."

"You killed Frizer?" he asked.

"No, we just sent him abroad for a while," Meg told him.

"But I still have Judith!" said Skeres.

She shook her head slowly.

"Frizer would never betray our secrets. There is no torture that would make him tell you that."

"Perhaps we found one," Meg said.

"Liar!"

Meg spoke to him like a reasonable mother talking to a wilful child. "She was in the loft above the stable at the Hanged Man. You chained her to the wall. I set her free about an hour ago. She will be well protected in future. You have no more power over us, Skeres. Give yourself up."

The knife moved as fast as a rat in his hand. I thought he was going to stab Meg and jumped forward, but he held the dagger over the sleeping playwright's heart. "I have all the power I want. Judith Shakespeare never mattered. Nor do you three. All I wanted was this villain Shakespeare in my power. I have that now. If you blink an eye, this knife goes through his heart."

"Why?" Meg asked.

"Because Master Shakespeare *has* to die. He is spreading Robert Cecil's message through his plays. It is not Her Majesty Queen Elizabeth's wish, so Master Shakespeare is a traitor. Traitors should be executed."

"But he is a great man!" Hugh cried. "Who knows what future works of genius you are destroying?"

"There have been greater playwrights," Skeres said. His calm mask was starting to crack.

"Like Marlowe?" Meg said suddenly.

He looked up at her with an expression of pain. "Like Marlowe," he agreed.

"The man your friend Frizer killed?" she asked. Meg moved forward and sat on the stone coffin lid beside him.

"That's right," he agreed.

"You want Shakespeare dead because he is becoming even greater than Marlowe. You can't bear the thought of Shakespeare writing those marvellous plays while Marlowe is forgotten."

"Perhaps," he admitted.

"Because Marlowe was a genius, and Marlowe was your friend," she said quietly.

"Yes," he said.

Meg looked at him until he lowered his glance to the figure in the shroud. "Liar," she whispered.

"What?"

"I said you are a *liar*. Marlowe was *not* your friend and you are *not* trying to protect his memory."

The knife trembled in Skeres's hand and I thought he was close to using it. "What do you mean?"

"I mean Master Shakespeare told us the story of the

◆ 184 ◆

death in Mrs Bull's tavern ten years ago."

"Nine years," the man said bitterly. "Nine long years."

"Nine years, then," Meg said with a shrug. "The story that everyone believes is that Marlowe was dozing on a bed, when he jumped up and attacked Frizer. Frizer defended himself and stabbed Marlowe in the eye. That's the story."

"And it's true," the man said.

"Here's another story," Meg said. "Marlowe was in deep trouble with the government. He was going on trial over some papers that were supposed to belong to him. Papers that showed he was a secret Catholic."

"Everyone knows that."

"Marlowe knew he faced trial and torture and a long spell in prison. His friend Thomas Kyd only lasted a year after he was released from that sort of treatment. Marlowe was desperate for a way out. That's when he met Skeres and Frizer in Mrs Bull's tavern. All day they tried to think of a way to help Marlowe. Maybe Skeres and Frizer weren't trying too hard. Maybe that's why Marlowe lost his temper and attacked Frizer."

"Maybe," the man agreed.

"And in the fight Marlowe was stabbed in the eye."

"He was."

"But, in *my* story, Marlowe didn't die. He lost his eye and he was unconscious. A doctor examined him and said he was dead, but the doctor made a mistake. In my story Skeres and Frizer saw Marlowe stir. They revived him. And they saw a way in which Marlowe could live on safely. Marlowe would be declared dead and the body of some plague victim could take his place in the coffin – it would be easy enough to arrange."

Skeres bowed his head slightly to one side. "And where is this Marlowe now?"

"It's just a story," Meg said.

"Then ... where is Marlowe in your story?"

"He changed his name, gave up the theatre where he would be recognized, and lived his life in the underworld of spies. It could have been done – a lot of the theatre people who knew him died in the plague. He was safe enough as long as he kept out of the Globe. But then he always knew that another actor had joined the spy trade. An actor and a writer called William Shakespeare. If Shakespeare ever met Marlowe through their new spy-lord Cecil, then he would recognize him. Marlowe's nine years of freedom would be over. Marlowe had to have Shakespeare killed."

The man half closed his eye. "So, this Kit Marlowe gave Frizer and me our orders."

"Not in my story," Meg said.

"So where is Marlowe now – in your story?"

Meg turned and looked at Hugh and at me. "Have you seen any one-eyed men around, Will? Hugh?" she asked.

"I only know one," I said quietly.

The man on the coffin looked up. "So, you think *I* am Kit Marlowe?"

"It makes sense. You know a lot about the theatre – *Romeo and Juliet* must have been performed at around the time of your tavern fight. You have only one eye because you were stabbed in the fight, but didn't die. You are keen to see Shakespeare dead – because you are jealous of his success and because he could recognize you. You took the name of Skeres when Skeres died shortly after your fight. Perhaps the real Skeres died of the plague. A lot of people in London did."

The man kept the knife in his right hand, but used his left to clap it softly. "A wonderful tale. You should be a playwright. *If* it is true – and, of course, it is a fantasy – *if* it is true then how will it end?"

"You must let Master Shakespeare live and then you

will be able to leave England," Meg said. "We'll even help you."

"And, if I don't?"

"Queen Elizabeth will die soon, and then your 'Skeres' name will be no protection. But, if you go *now*, you can join your friend Frizer in France. Maybe you'll get a pardon one day and be able to return to England."

"I could still kill Master Shakespeare first?"

"There would be no need. He doesn't know your secret – he never will, unless you are still around when he wakes up and sees you."

"*You* know my secret."

"You don't need to kill us either. We're harmless ... a boy, a girl and a bag-of-wind actor. Go now, Kit. Go now while you *can*. Ingram Frizer will have landed at Caen by now. You can join him." Meg pulled her purse out from inside her doublet. "Mistress Shakespeare is offering you ten pounds to help you start again in France."

His eye glowed in the amber light of the lantern. Out in the graveyard the autumn wind stirred and rattled the yew trees. Inside the crypt it was silent. Silent as the grave, in fact.

Slowly the man who called himself Skeres raised the dagger and placed it carefully in his belt. "If Kit Marlowe had lived, then he would have been a greater writer than William Shakespeare, you know," he said.

"That's what everyone in the theatre says," Hugh Richmond agreed.

The spy looked up with an expression of pain mixed with pride. "They do?"

"I've played Kit Marlowe's *Doctor Faustus* myself," the actor said. "Wonderful poetry – magnificent theatre. What a loss poor Marlowe's disappearance was."

"Ah, Faustus." The man reached out and took the purse of gold Meg held, then rose to his feet. He walked to the entrance of the crypt and looked into the night sky. "Faustus was the story of a man who sold his soul to the devil and tried too late to claim it back."

Meg rose and stood behind him. "It's never too late. We can all change the way we live ... if we really want to."

"Can we?"

"You *could* have killed Master Shakespeare before we arrived and escaped easily. But you *didn't*. Maybe that's because you've already begun to change," I said.

The light of the lantern barely lit his face as he turned to look at us one last time, yet I'll swear I saw a tear in that diamond-hard, glittering eye. He pulled his dark cloak around him and stepped into the blackness of the churchyard. He vanished as suddenly as a snuffed out candleflame.

"Was that the great Kit Marlowe?" Hugh asked.

"There are some mysteries that were never meant to be solved," Meg told him.

CHAPTER NINETEEN

"The rest is silence"

MEG LUMLEY'S STORY

I agreed to tell my half of Will Marsden's story, if he would let me have the last word. I think that's fair. In our world men have all *other* words, so it's only fair that we women should have the *last*. Anne Shakespeare taught me that.

Will is modest. He makes it sound as if my cleverness saved the great playwright's life. I guessed that Marlowe had disguised himself as Skeres. He was ready to kill Master Shakespeare to protect his secret. Once I told him I knew his secret, then there was no need to kill him ... unless he was going to kill us all. But, as Titus Andronicus discovered, there is only so much blood and terror one person can bear.

Perhaps I was right. Or perhaps Nicholas Skeres was Nicholas Skeres and Christopher Marlowe was dead. Whichever it was, you have to admit it was Will's courage in entering the crypt that really saved Master Shakespeare.

Will's courage or my cleverness? What does it matter? We are all made of dreams and our little life ends with a sleep.

A sleep. That autumn morning we carried the play-

wright back to New Place and left him in the care of his wife. We lay down on the fine beds and slept. Like the dead. Even the drugged playwright was awake before us!

He had a large bandage wrapped around his thumb where his enemy-friend had sliced it. He introduced his bright-eyed daughter, Judith, to Will, and the boy blushed when faced with such beauty. (Though he says this is not true.) He should have seen her as I found her in the hay loft; fear and hunger change people.

Master Shakespeare asked what had happened in the crypt the night before while he had slept. For some reason neither Will nor Hugh wanted to tell him about Marlowe ... an old friend turned murderer is just too cruel to bear. "When Skeres saw you were dead, and when we told him we had set Judith free, he gave up. I think he went to seek his fortune in the Americas," I lied.

That story satisfied the Shakespeare family. Master Shakespeare went on with his writing. "The Queen will need a new play for the Christmas season – if she lives that long," he explained. "We'll meet the company at the Globe in November when the sweating sickness is gone from London."

"We can't stay here till then," Will said.

"Of course you can," Anne said. "You are very welcome."

"Will's right," I agreed. "We can go home to Marsden Manor for a few weeks, then travel down to London on one of the coal ships. Everyone in Marsden will want to know what happened after we left."

We spent the day arguing with our host and hostess, but in the end they gave us two fine horses as a reward for our help and more than enough money to stay in the best inns on the road home.

On the morning we left Master Shakespeare placed a script in Will's hands. "Learn your part so you are ready to start rehearsing a month from now," he said.

Will stowed it carefully in his saddle pack, but never opened it until we reached Marsden Manor a week later.

The Marsden family were pleased to see us. "Give us one of those fine speeches from the Globe plays," Great-Uncle George demanded as we sat round the fireplace in the hall after dinner one night.

Autumn winds had stripped the trees almost bare out-side and the leaves rattled against the windows. Draughts made the tapestries on the walls tremble, but it was warm enough around the fire. This was the best time of the day.

The time when the family told its old stories. Tales of terror and times long gone, of people long dead. Now Will and I had our own story to tell. We had listened to the tale and taken our pleasure. It was good to be able to give something back. A tale of a night in a crypt with a killer and a playwright who rose from the dead ... or, if I was right, *two* playwrights who had risen from the dead.

"I could try out one of my speeches from Master Shakespeare's newest play. The one we'll act before the Queen at Richmond Palace this Christmas."

"Hah!" Grandfather cried and rubbed his dry old hands together. "We are going to be the first people to hear a new Shakespeare play! What an honour!"

Grandmother chuckled. "And we'll hear it before that little witch, Elizabeth."

"That's right," Will laughed, and the fire crackled while the light sparkled in his simple boyish eyes.

"Is it a good play? As good as that *Titus* thing?" his father asked.

"It has a good title," I said. "In fact, the title could hardly be better!"

"What's that?" Lady Marsden asked in her gentle way.

Will told her. "*All's Well that Ends Well!*"

The Historical Characters

The Marsden family are fictional, but several of the characters really did exist:

WILLIAM SHAKESPEARE 1564-1616 Shakespeare is the writer of some of the greatest plays in the English language, yet not a great deal is known about his life. He married Anne Hathaway (d. 1623) and had a daughter, Susanna, and twins, Judith and Hamnet. Hamnet died in 1596 at the age of 11. William Shakespeare left Stratford and became rich as a playwright, actor and theatre owner in London. Still he seems to have been a loyal "family" man. He visited Stratford regularly, but especially in the summer months when plague closed The Globe Theatre in London. Some modern historians believe he may have been a spy for the Queen's government.

CHRISTOPHER MARLOWE 1564–1593 Christopher Marlowe, known as Kit, went to Cambridge University where he learned about playwriting. He was also recruited by Elizabeth's ministers as a spy. He took his writing skills to London where his plays were hugely popular, but writing plays never made him much money and spying became an important way of making a living. Kit was hot-tempered and often in trouble with the law. It's not too surprising that his life ended violently in a knife fight. But it is possible that the "death" was faked to get him out of trouble. Many people seriously believe he lived on and wrote plays using Shakespeare's name. No one has considered the possibility explored in this story – that he lived on, but *didn't* write any more plays. He simply continued as a spy.

INGRAM FRIZER AND NICHOLAS SKERES The two men who were present at the death of Kit Marlowe. They gave the magistrates the story of Marlowe attacking Frizer and being fatally wounded in the scuffle. The trouble is that they were such lying rogues, you shouldn't believe anything they said! We know little about their lives, but they made a dishonest living from moneylending and thieving. Skeres was one of the spies who worked for the government to trap Mary Queen of Scots. As a result of his work she was beheaded.

The Time Trail

1564 (February) Christopher Marlowe is born in Canterbury, the son of a shoemaker.

1564 (April) William Shakespeare is born in Stratfordupon-Avon, the son of a glovemaker.

1586 Mary Queen of Scots is brought to trial and sentenced to death, thanks to a plot against her. A spy for Elizabeth, Nicholas Skeres, was one of the plotters. Mary is executed early the following year.

1587 At about this time Shakespeare moves to London to write plays and act. He is soon a success as an actor.

c. 1590–2 Shakespeare writes his first play, *The Two Gentlemen of Verona*, while Kit Marlowe's *Jew of Malta* is already a huge success.

1592 The plague closes all London theatres for the first time. Shakespeare writes poetry instead of plays and it is extremely popular.

1593 Kit Marlowe is killed in Mrs Bull's tavern in Deptford, London. It is said he argued with two spies, Frizer and Skeres, about the bill for their meal.

1599 The Globe Theatre opens with William Shakespeare as one of the owners.

1601 The Earl of Essex leads a rebellion to take control of Elizabeth I's government. It fails and he is beheaded. William Shakespeare's actors are blamed for performing *Richard II* – the story of a successful rebellion – to encourage the plotters.

1603 Elizabeth I dies.

1611 Shakespeare writes his last great play, *The Tempest*, and seems to have retired to Stratford.

1616 William Shakespeare dies in Stratford at the age of 52.

Tudor Terror

The Prince of Rags and Patches

A visitor comes to Marsden Manor, bearing letters from the dying Queen Elizabeth to James VI of Scotland.

A man lies dead in Bournmoor Woods – murdered.

And Will Marsden, aided and abetted by Meg the serving girl, sets out to find the killer.

Meanwhile Will is puzzling over the story of his Marsden ancestor who followed Richard II into battle, was mixed up in the mysterious deaths of the Princes in the Tower ... and whose meeting with a prince of rags and patches gives Will the clue he needs.

Two parallel stories of murder and intrigue, each building to a thrilling climax!

·Nemo · me · impune·

Tudor Terror

The King in Blood Red and Gold

When handsome, foppish Hugh Richmond turns up at Marsden Manor, claiming to be one of Queen Elizabeth's spies and asking for help, Will and his grandfather seize on the chance for adventure!

Riding north to Scotland, Grandfather tells Will he fought at the Battle of Flodden Field in the service of Henry VIII. Then as now, there were desperate skirmishes on the Borders between the English and the Scots Reivers – cattle thieves.

Neither of them realize quite what danger Hugh is leading them into ... and it seems that all their courage and quick wit will not get them out.

Luckily, Meg the serving girl is very clever ...

Two interwoven stories of battle and adventure, each as exciting as the other.

The Lady of Fire and Tears

A silver cup has been stolen from Marsden Hall and Meg the serving girl will hang for it.

Unless she agrees to spy on her friends at the Black Bull Tavern ...

For loyal Meg it is a terrible dilemma. Her friend Will is desperate to save her. And Will's mother decides to tell them the story she has kept secret for so many years ... how she herself, as a young lady-in-waiting, was forced to spy on Mary Queen of Scots.

Two stories of spies and double-dealing are brilliantly intertwined in a thrilling drama.

The Knight of Stars and Storms

The Marsden family are in desperate trouble. If they can't pay their debts, they will lose their home.

So Will and his father, Sir James – and Meg the serving girl who refuses to be left behind – set sail for London with a cargo of coal to sell, to save the family fortunes.

But someone is out to get them ...

And it is only when Sir James recounts his adventures sailing the Pacific with Sir Francis Drake twenty-five years before that Will and Meg are able to work out a plan of action.

Pirates, spies and sea captains feature in a tale of nailbiting suspense and excitement.